JAKE MADDOX
GRAPHIC NOVELS

BASKETBALL CAMP CHAMP

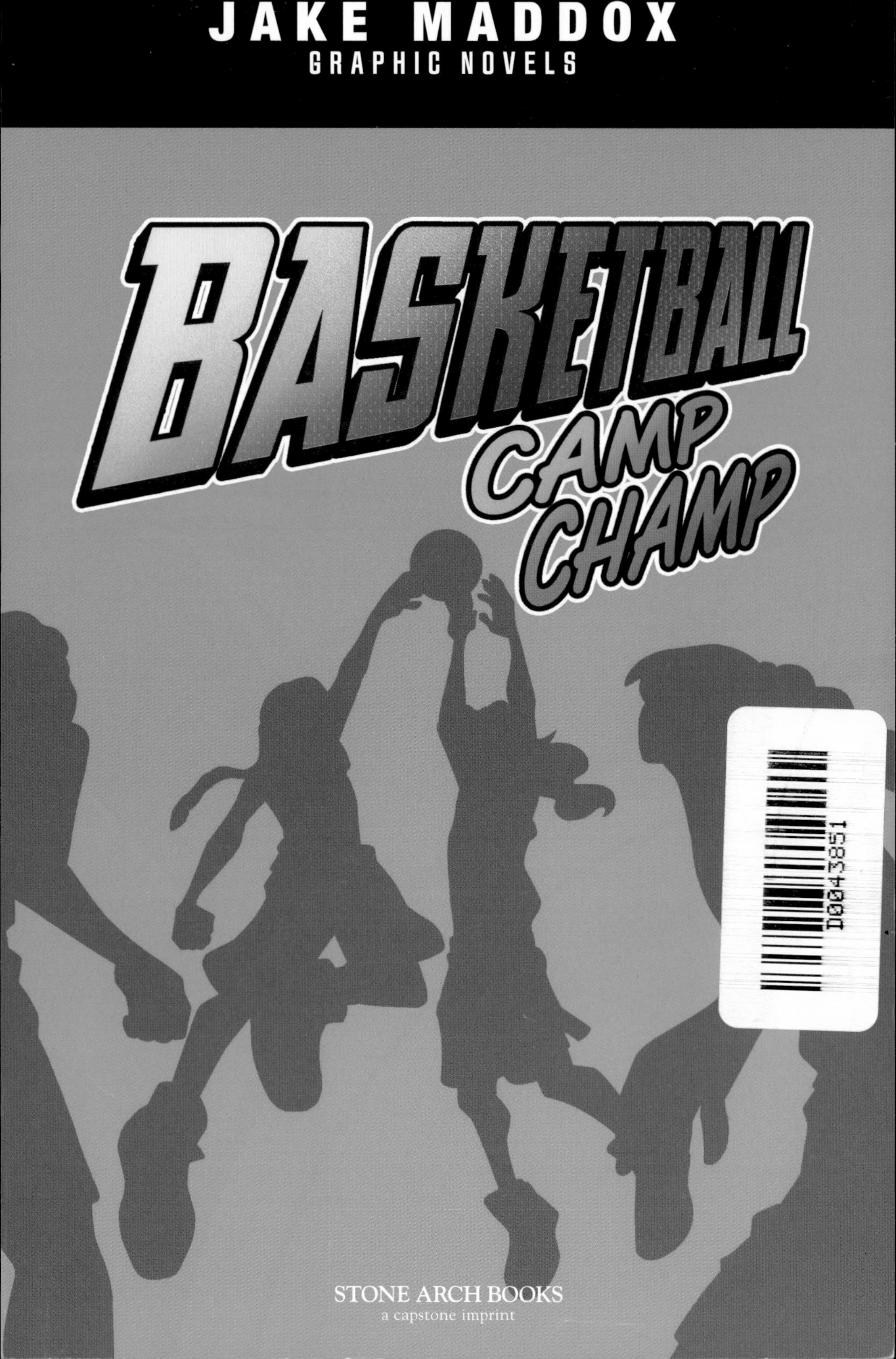

STONE ARCH BOOKS
a capstone imprint

JAKE MADDOX
GRAPHIC NOVELS

Published by Stone Arch Books,
an imprint of Capstone.
1710 Roe Crest Drive
North Mankato, Minnesota 56003
www.capstonepub.com

Library of Congress Cataloging-in-Publication Data
is available on the Library of Congress website.

ISBN: 978-1-4965-8375-8 (library binding)
ISBN: 978-1-4965-8454-0 (paperback)
ISBN: 978-1-4965-8380-2 (ebook PDF)

Summary: After only ever playing pickup
games, Ana is excited to attend a basketball
summer camp where she'll play on a real team.
But when the coach says they'll use something
called "zone defense," the shooting guard feels
lost and starts to doubt her skills. Can Ana get
out of her comfort zone and ask for help?

Designed by Brann Garvey

Printed in the United States of America.
PA100

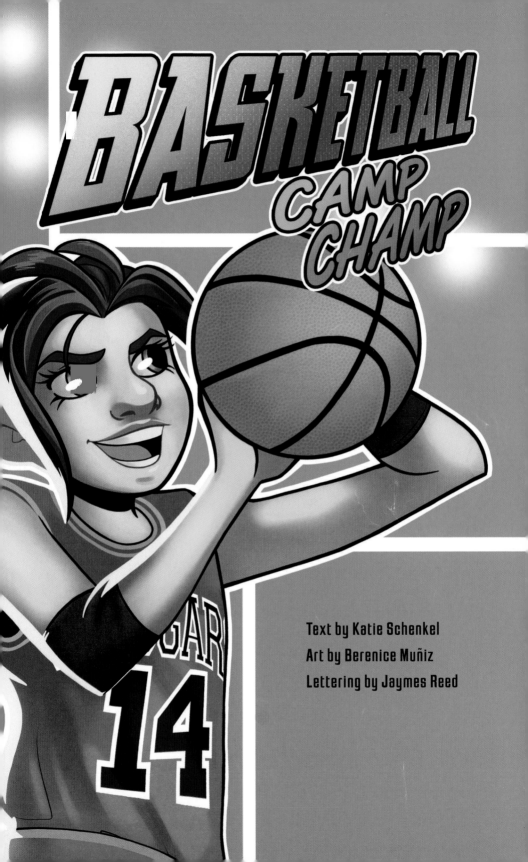

BASKETBALL
CAMP CHAMP

Text by Katie Schenkel
Art by Berenice Muñiz
Lettering by Jaymes Reed

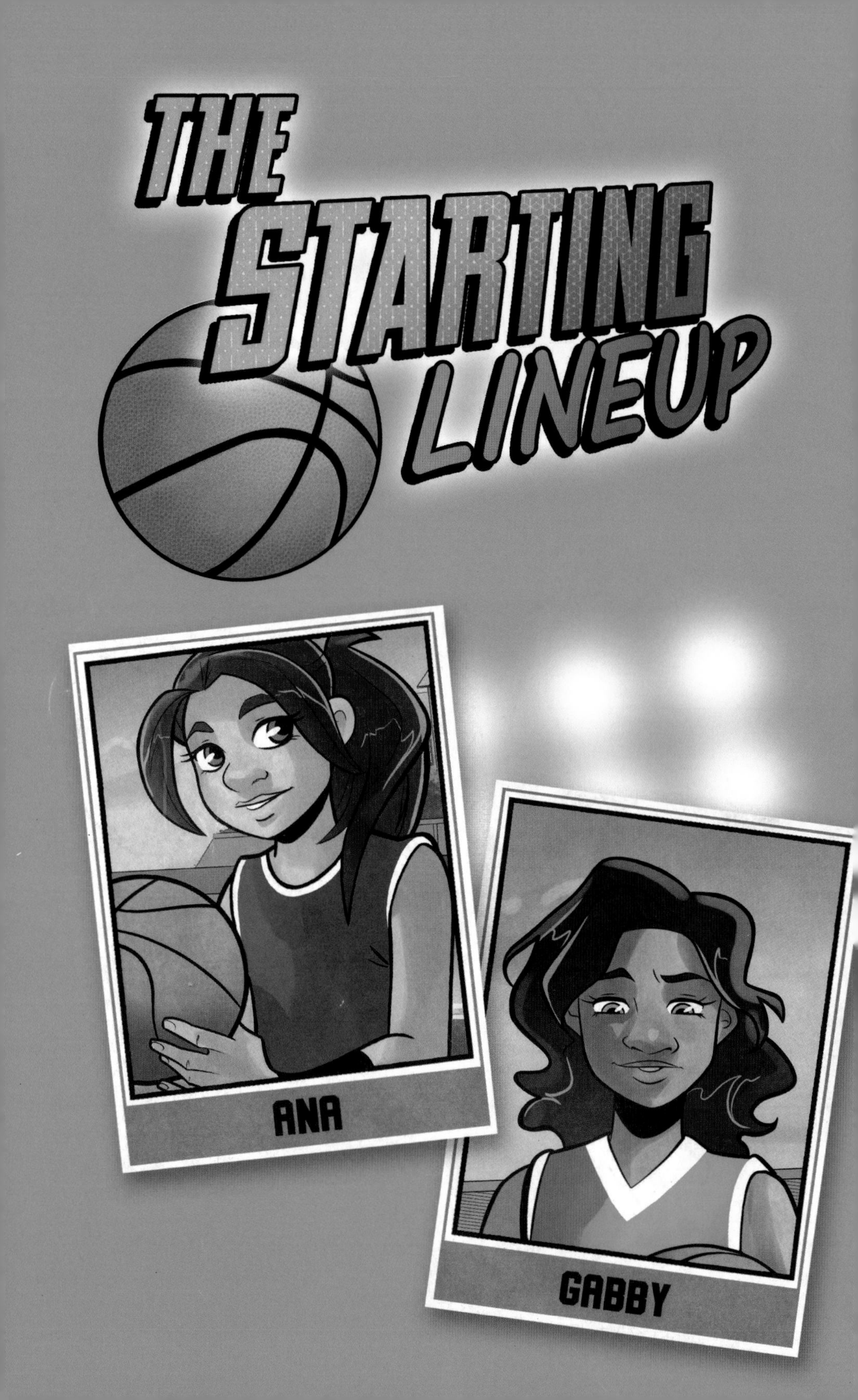
THE STARTING LINEUP
ANA
GABBY

NICOLE

KIMBRA AND KYLIE

COACH PAM

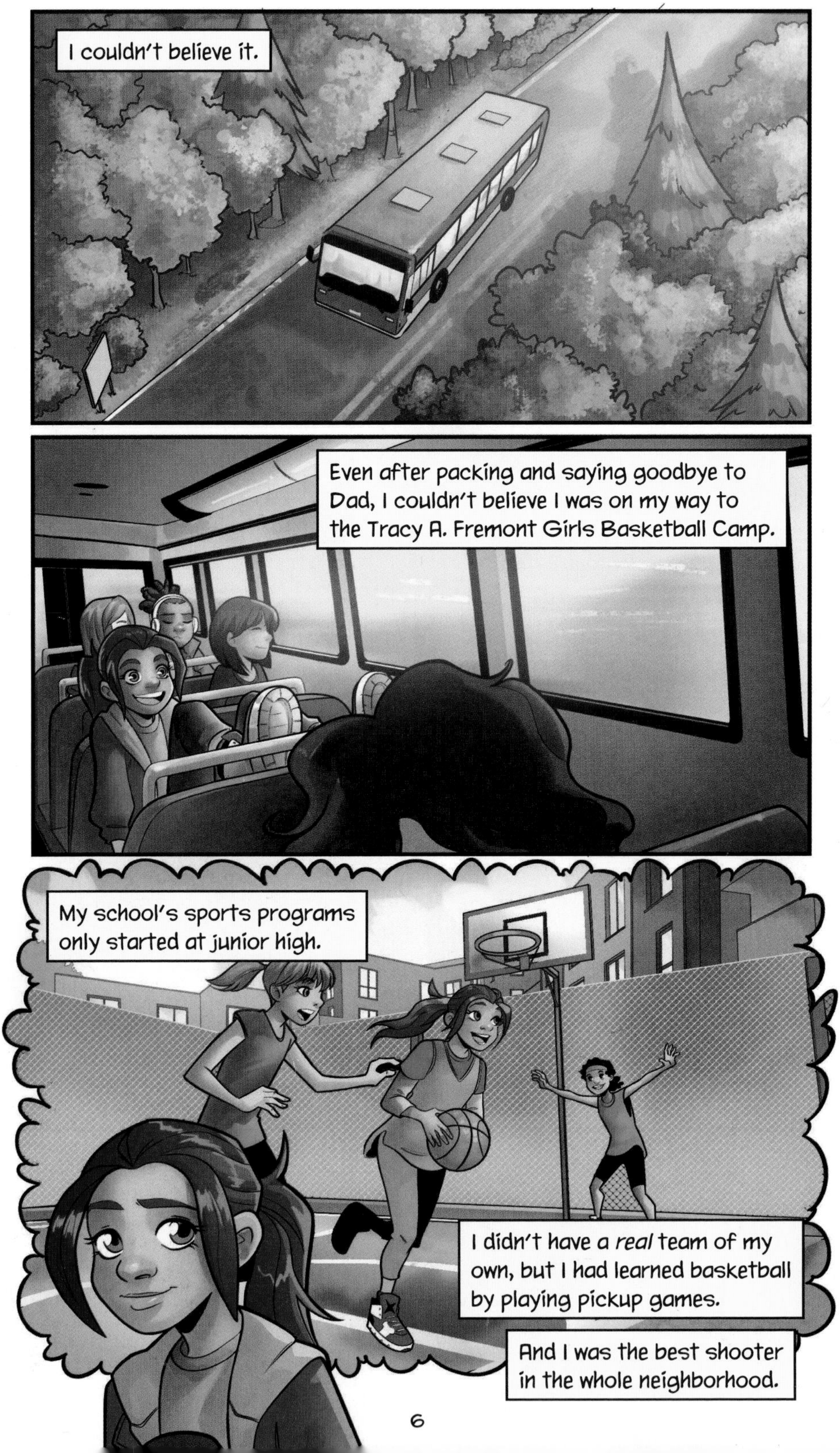
I couldn't believe it.
Even after packing and saying goodbye to Dad, I couldn't believe I was on my way to the Tracy A. Fremont Girls Basketball Camp.
My school's sports programs only started at junior high.
I didn't have a *real* team of my own, but I had learned basketball by playing pickup games.
And I was the best shooter in the whole neighborhood.

When Dad convinced me to sign up for the big city-wide free throw contest, I never thought I'd win.

FREE THROW CONTEST

But I did.

And I got the grand prize—a full scholarship to a real basketball camp.

TRACY A. FREMONT GIRLS BASKETBALL CAMP

-Games & Tournament
-Focus and Fun
-Expert Coaching
-Teamwork

No cell phone, no computers, no distractions. Just four weeks of serious training.

I was going to have a *real* coach and a *real* team and—

Excuse me.

KICK!

KICK!

KICK!

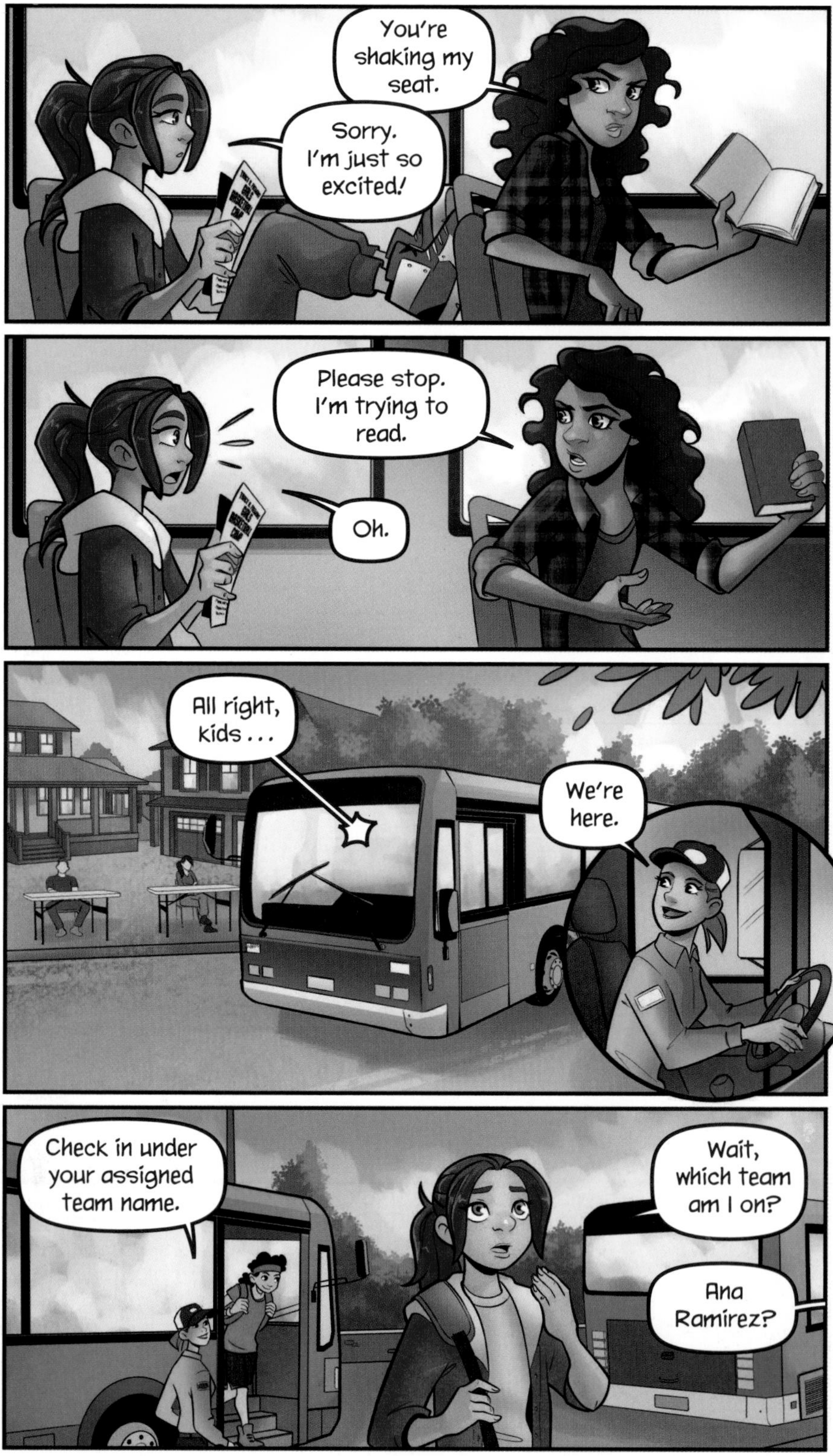

You're shaking my seat.
Sorry. I'm just so excited!
Please stop. I'm trying to read.
Oh.
All right, kids . . .
We're here.
Check in under your assigned team name.
Wait, which team am I on?
Ana Ramirez?

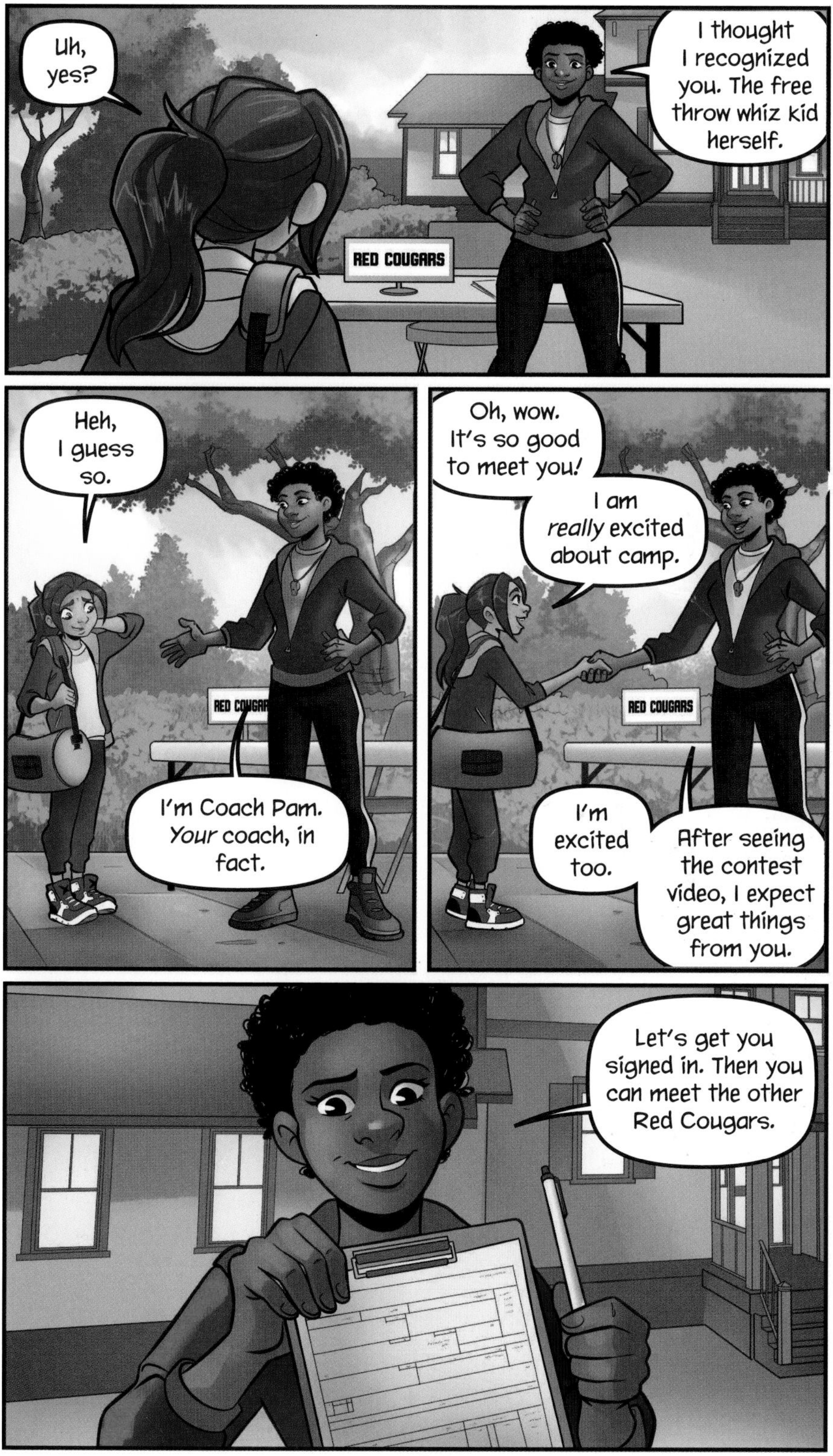
Uh, yes?
I thought I recognized you. The free throw whiz kid herself.
RED COUGARS
Heh, I guess so.
I'm Coach Pam. *Your* coach, in fact.
Oh, wow. It's so good to meet you!
I am *really* excited about camp.
RED COUGARS
I'm excited too.
After seeing the contest video, I expect great things from you.
Let's get you signed in. Then you can meet the other Red Cougars.

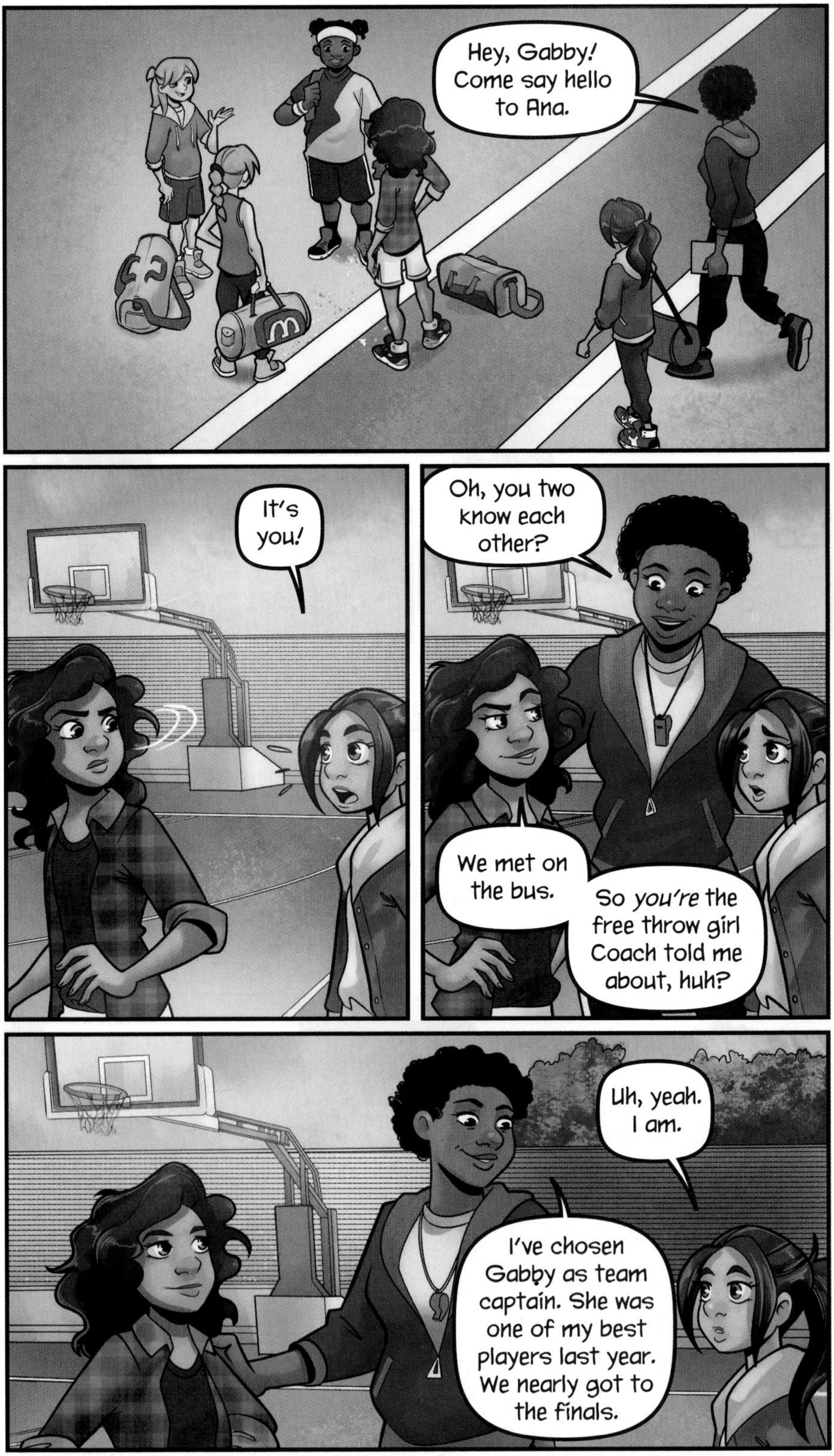
Hey, Gabby! Come say hello to Ana.
It's you!
Oh, you two know each other?
We met on the bus.
So you're the free throw girl Coach told me about, huh?
Uh, yeah. I am.
I've chosen Gabby as team captain. She was one of my best players last year. We nearly got to the finals.

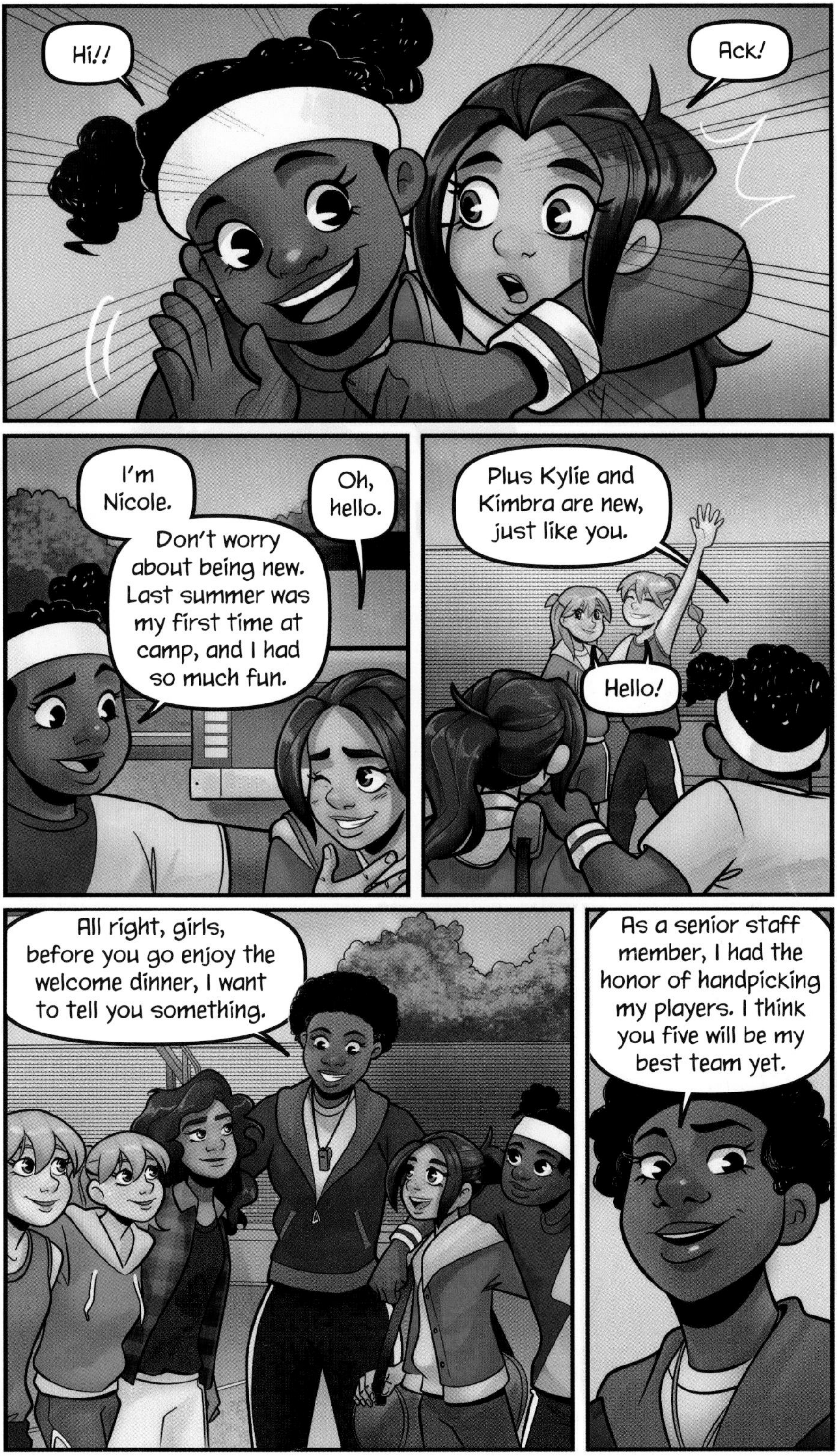
Hi!!
Ack!
I'm Nicole.
Don't worry about being new. Last summer was my first time at camp, and I had so much fun.
Oh, hello.
Plus Kylie and Kimbra are new, just like you.
Hello!
All right, girls, before you go enjoy the welcome dinner, I want to tell you something.
As a senior staff member, I had the honor of handpicking my players. I think you five will be my best team yet.

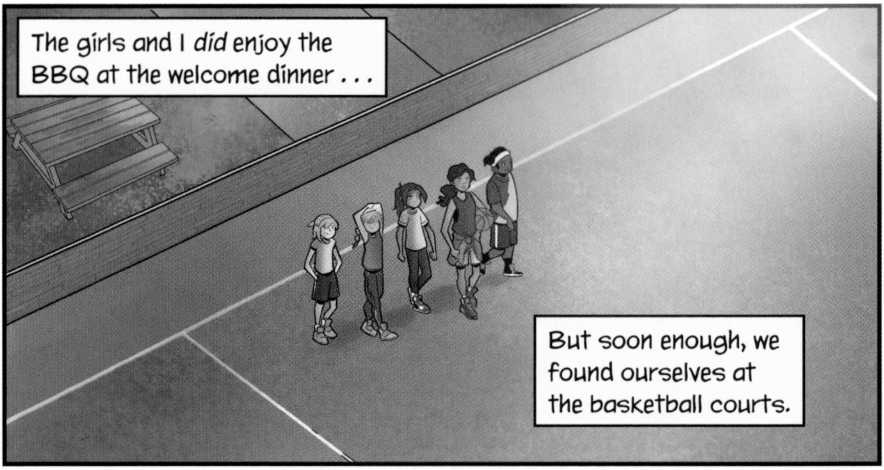
The girls and I *did* enjoy the BBQ at the welcome dinner . . .
But soon enough, we found ourselves at the basketball courts.

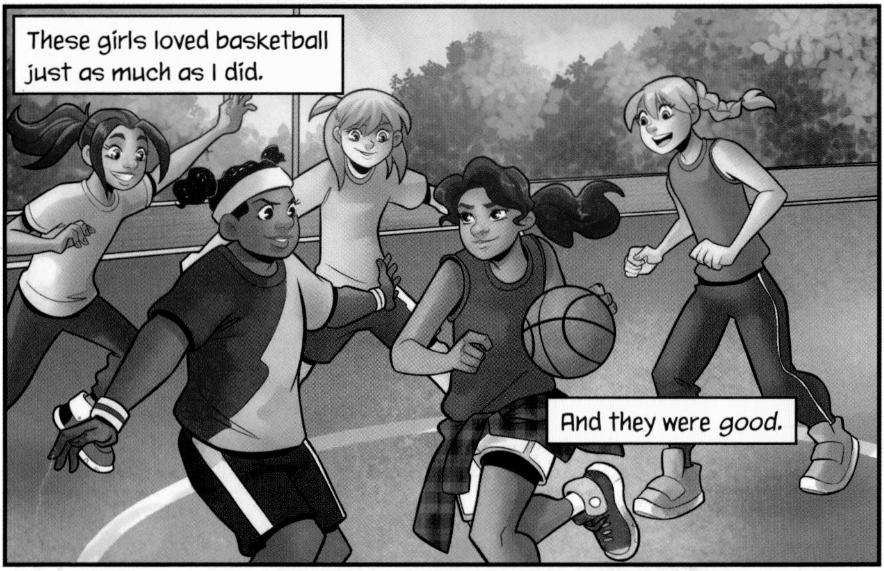
These girls loved basketball just as much as I did.
And they were *good.*

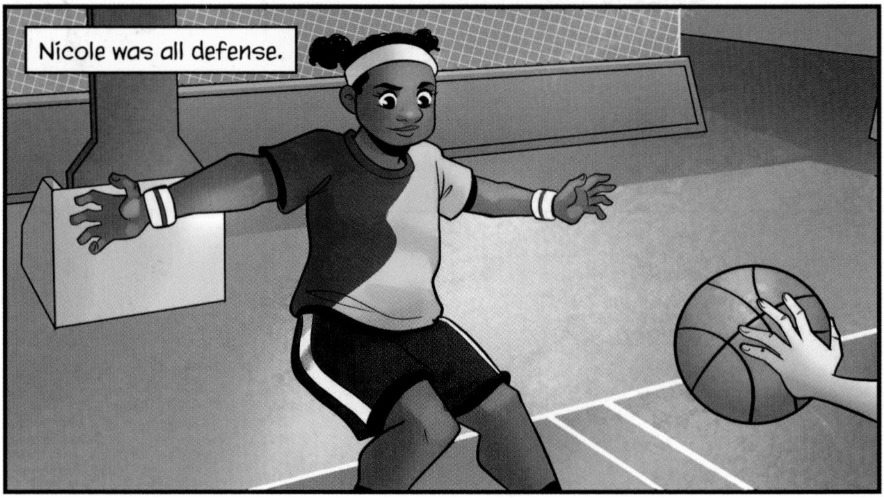
Nicole was all defense.

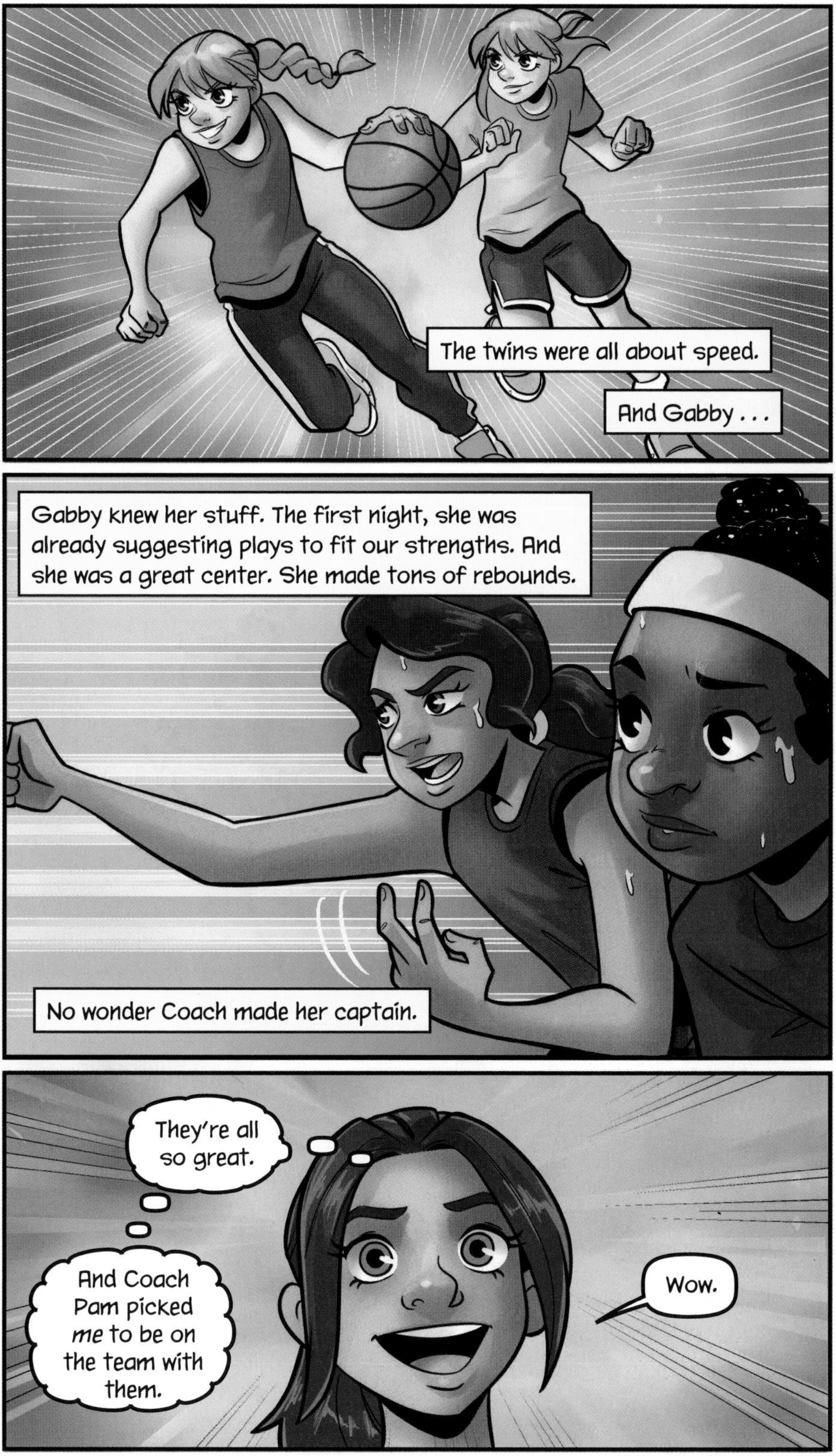
The twins were all about speed.
And Gabby . . .
Gabby knew her stuff. The first night, she was already suggesting plays to fit our strengths. And she was a great center. She made tons of rebounds.
No wonder Coach made her captain.
They're all so great.
And Coach Pam picked *me* to be on the team with them.
Wow.

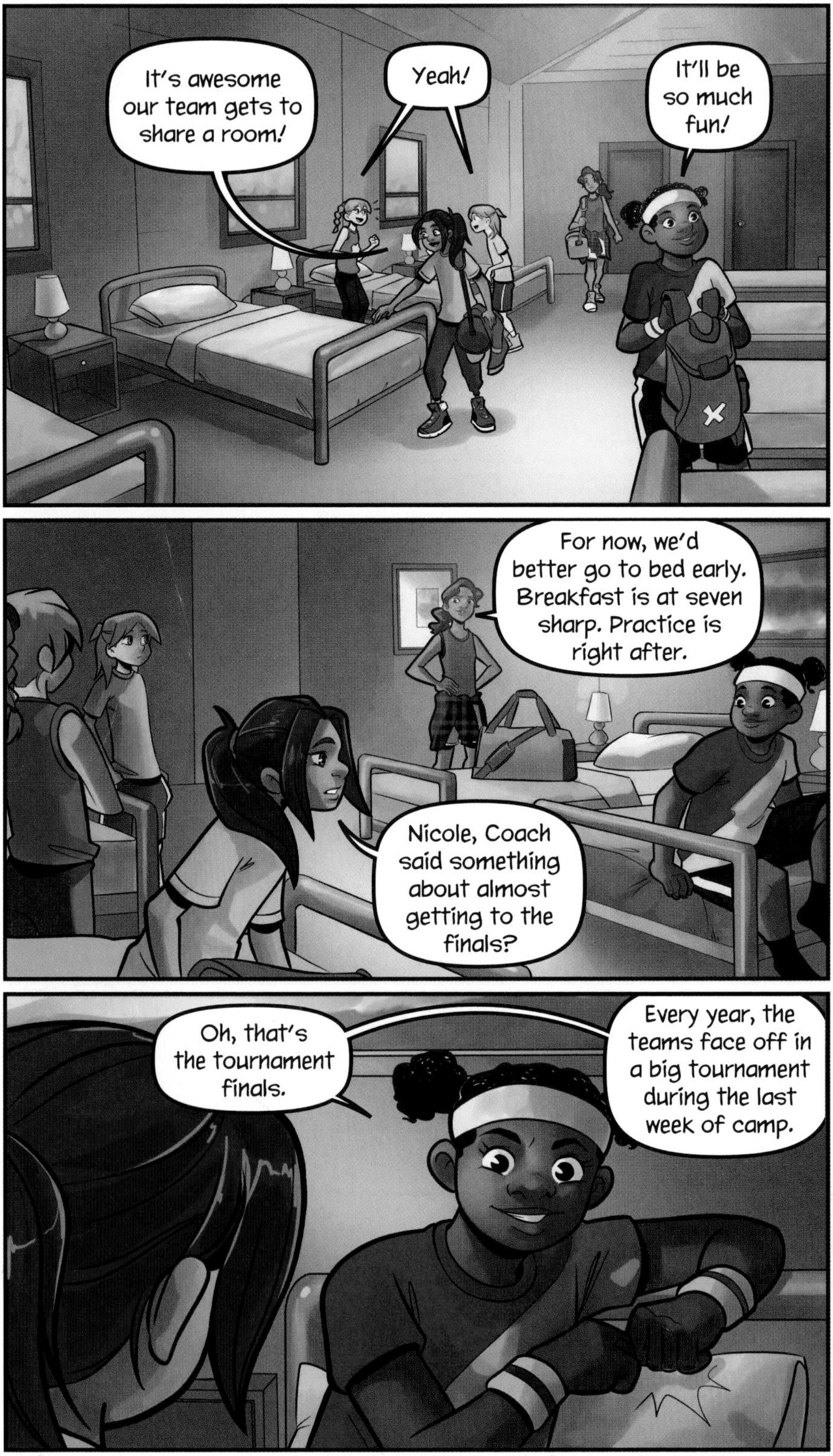
It's awesome our team gets to share a room!
Yeah!
It'll be so much fun!
For now, we'd better go to bed early. Breakfast is at seven sharp. Practice is right after.
Nicole, Coach said something about almost getting to the finals?
Oh, that's the tournament finals.
Every year, the teams face off in a big tournament during the last week of camp.

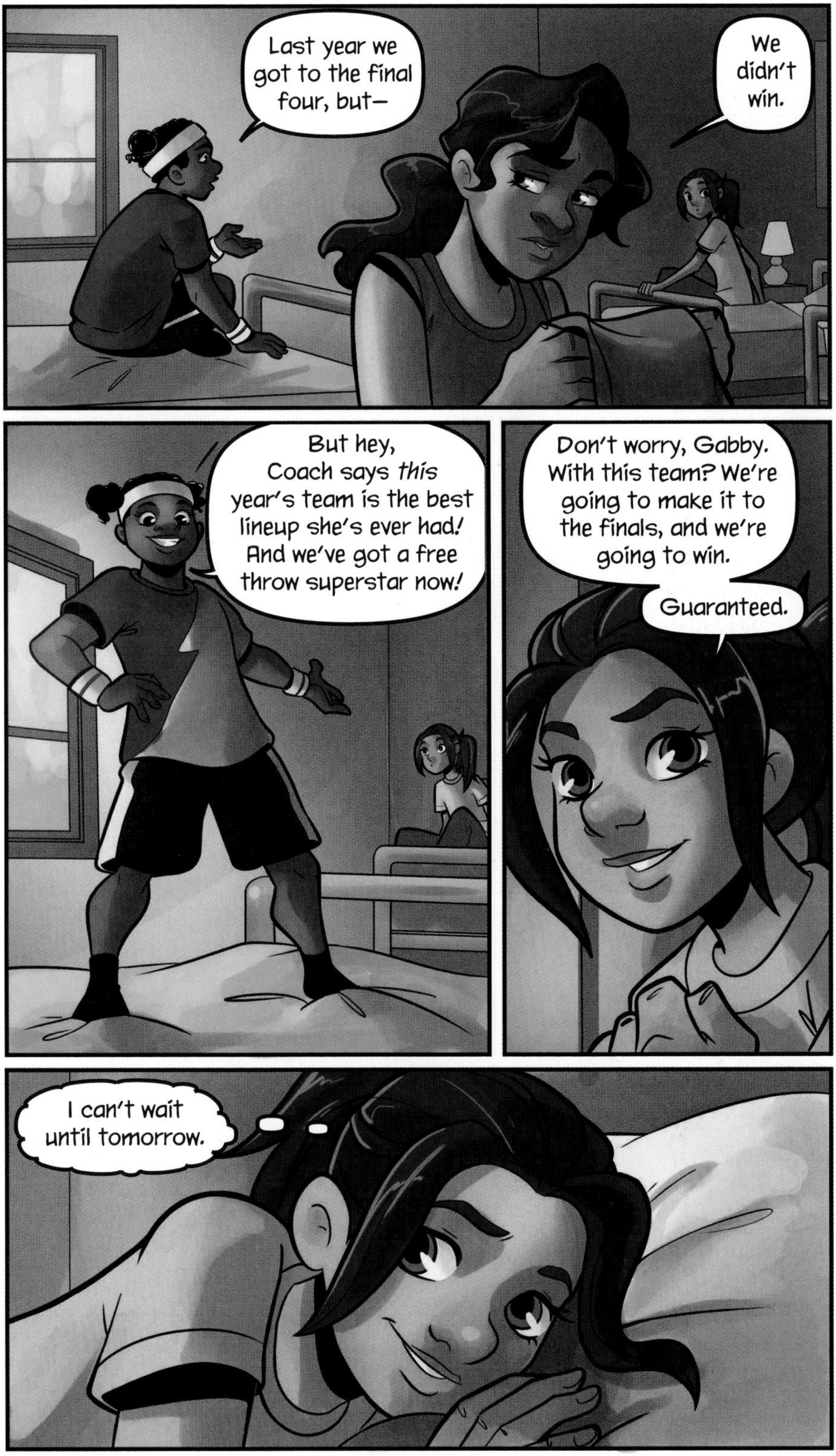
Last year we got to the final four, but—
We didn't win.
But hey, Coach says *this* year's team is the best lineup she's ever had! And we've got a free throw superstar now!
Don't worry, Gabby. With this team? We're going to make it to the finals, and we're going to win.
Guaranteed.
I can't wait until tomorrow.

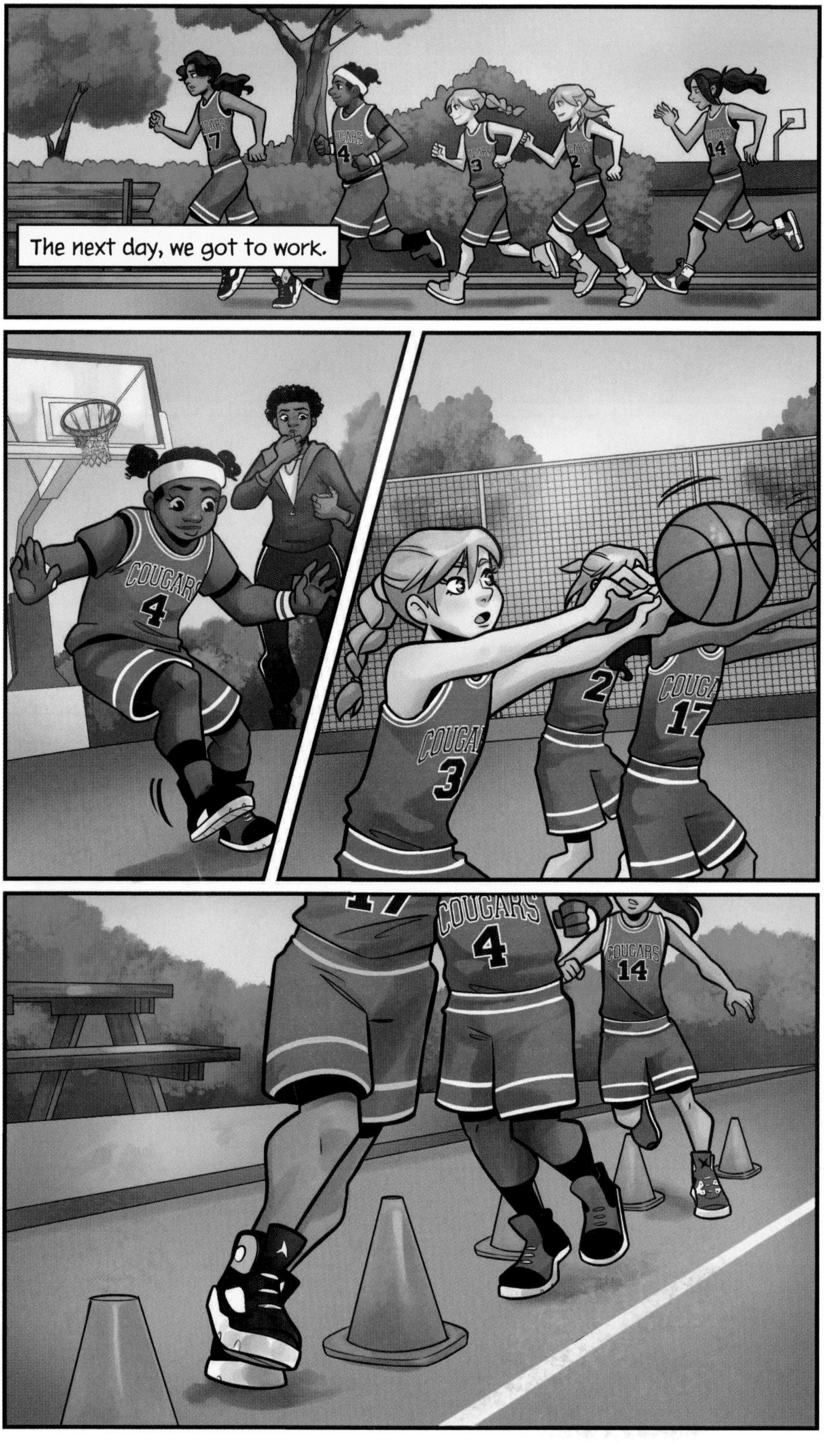
The next day, we got to work.

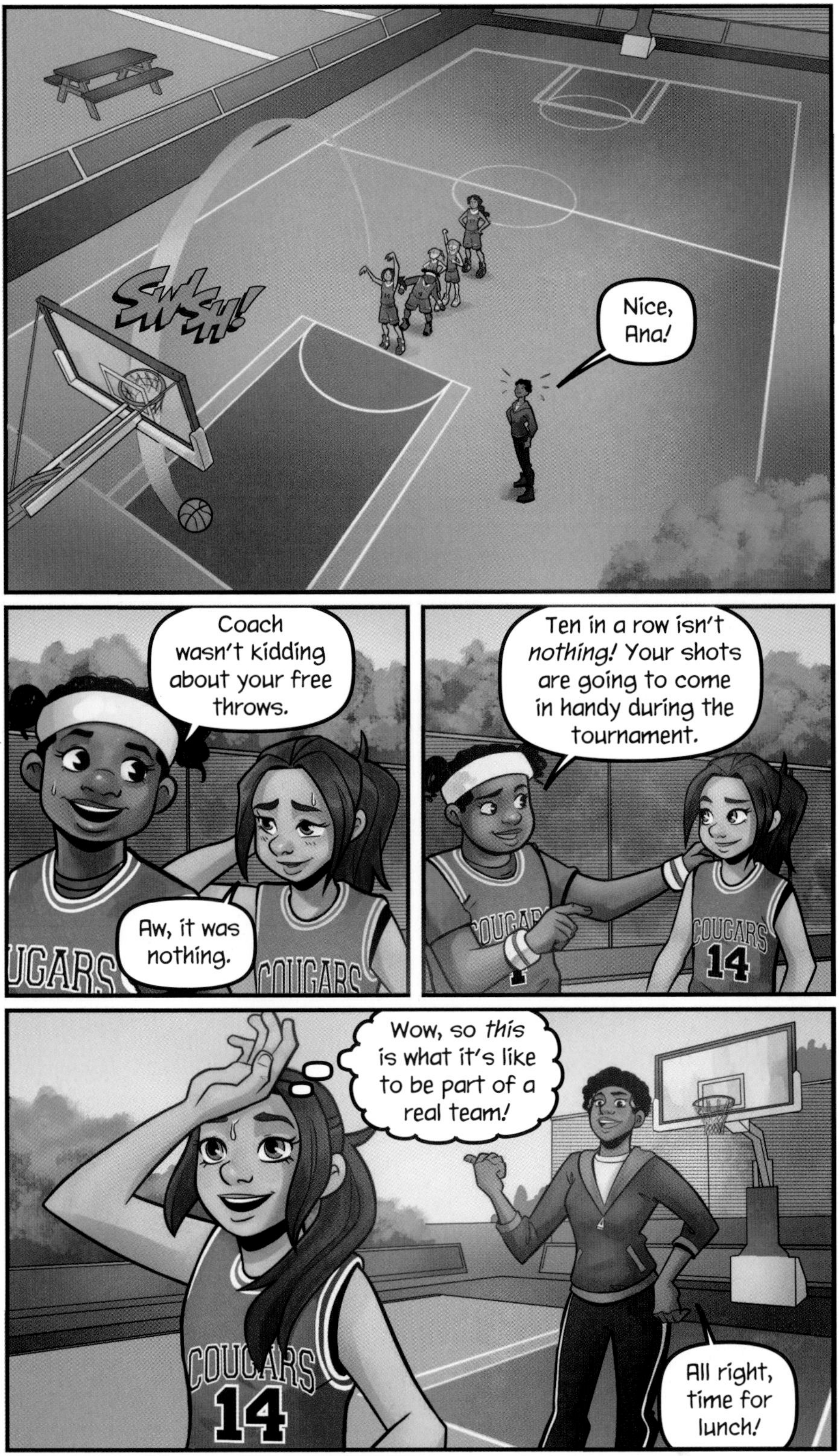
SWISH!
Nice, Ana!
Coach wasn't kidding about your free throws.
Aw, it was nothing.
Ten in a row isn't *nothing!* Your shots are going to come in handy during the tournament.
Wow, so *this* is what it's like to be part of a real team!
All right, time for lunch!

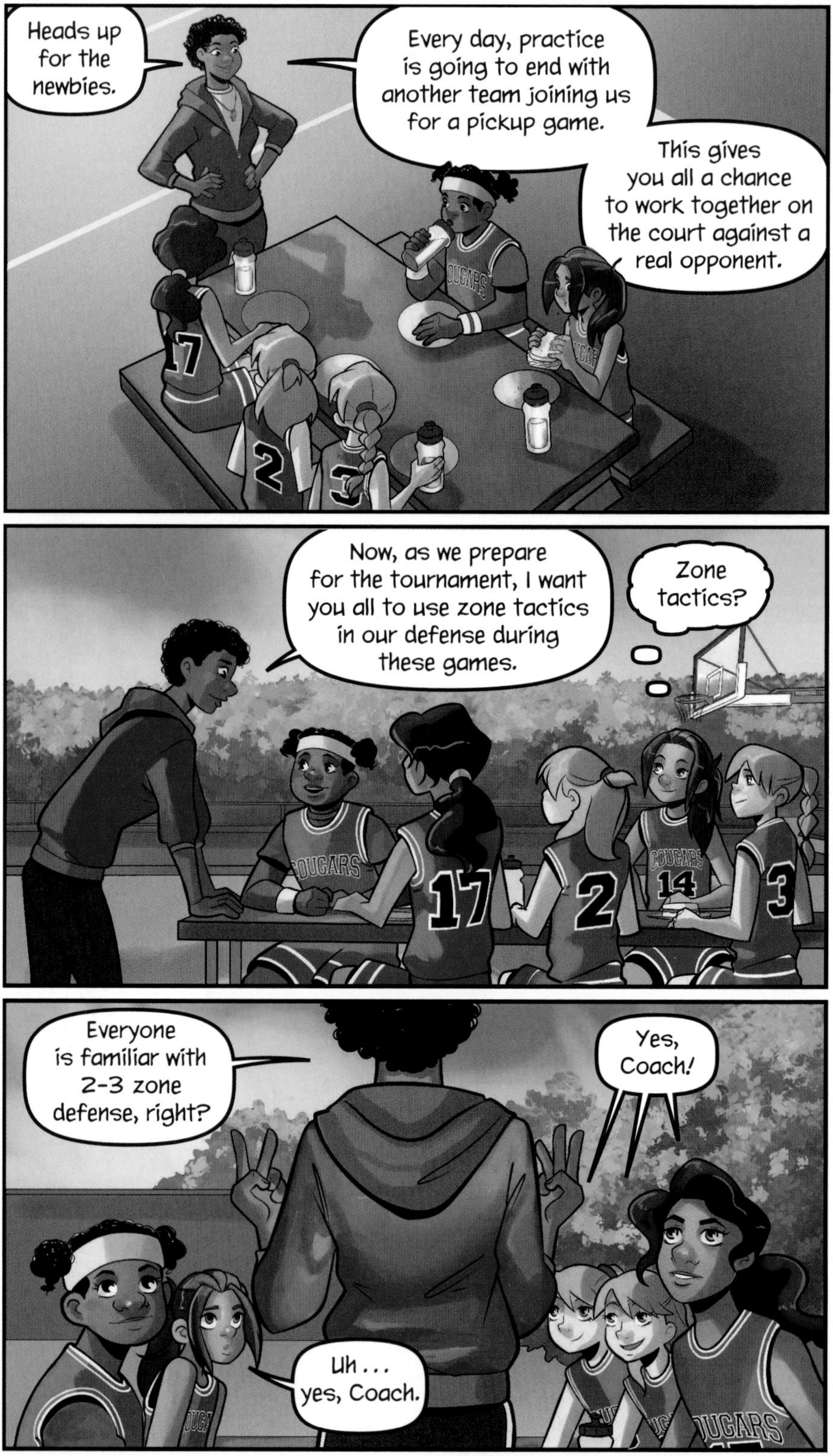
Heads up for the newbies.
Every day, practice is going to end with another team joining us for a pickup game.
This gives you all a chance to work together on the court against a real opponent.
17
COUGARS
2
3
Now, as we prepare for the tournament, I want you all to use zone tactics in our defense during these games.
Zone tactics?
COUGARS
17
2
COUGARS
14
3
Everyone is familiar with 2-3 zone defense, right?
Yes, Coach!
Uh . . . yes, Coach.
COUGARS

So for today, I want Nicole to—

Why did I say I knew what she's talking about?!

But everyone already thinks I'm a great player.

If I ask Coach now, the girls will think I'm a phony.

What am I going to do?

Everyone know their positions?

Yes, Coach!

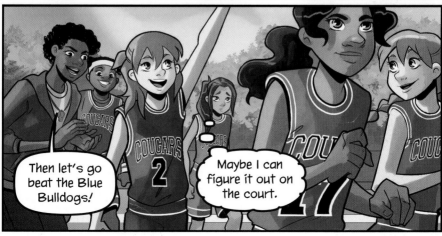

Then let's go beat the Blue Bulldogs!

Maybe I can figure it out on the court.

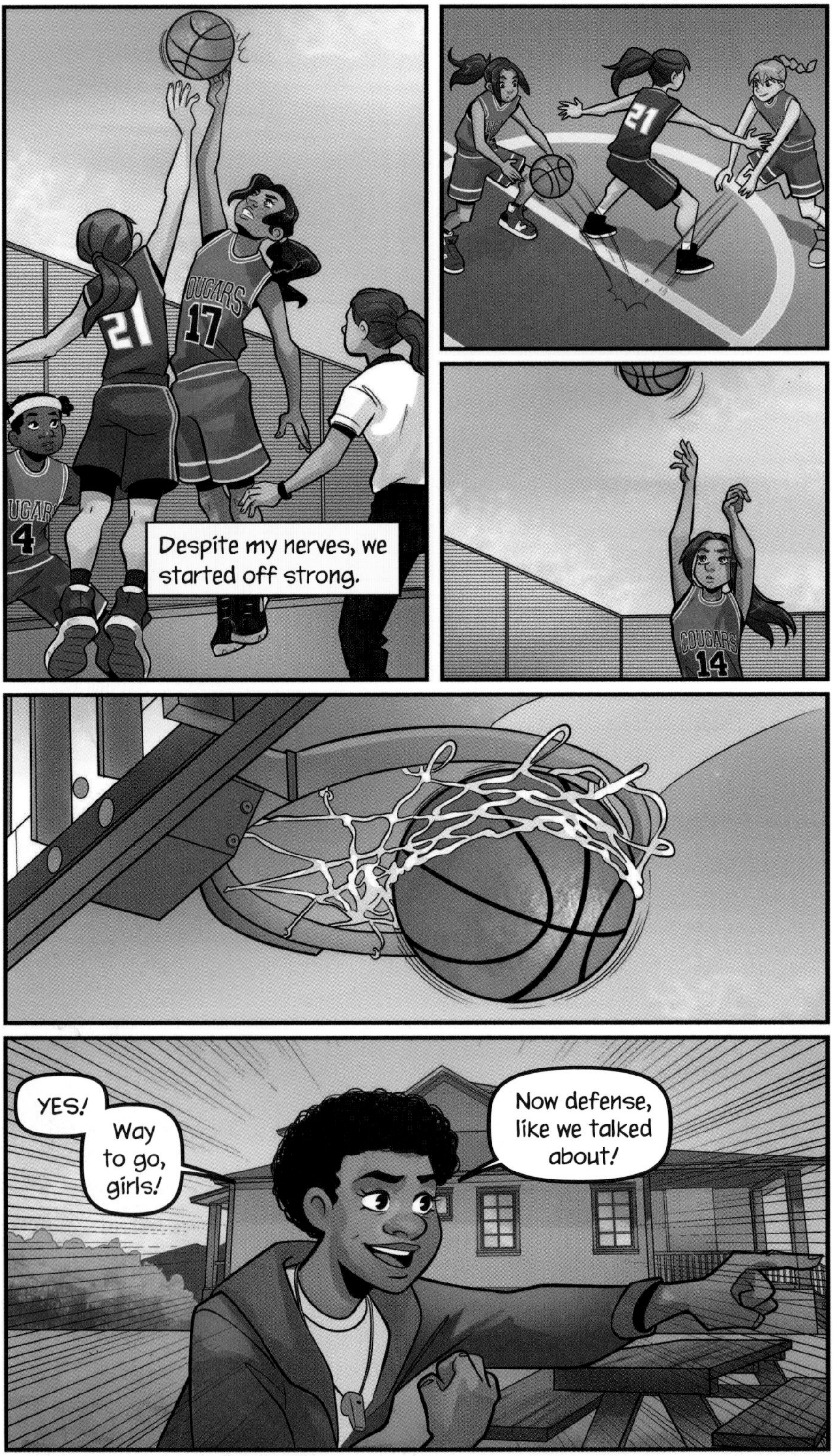
COUGARS
21
17
COUGARS
4
Despite my nerves, we started off strong.
21
COUGARS
14
YES!
Way to go, girls!
Now defense, like we talked about!

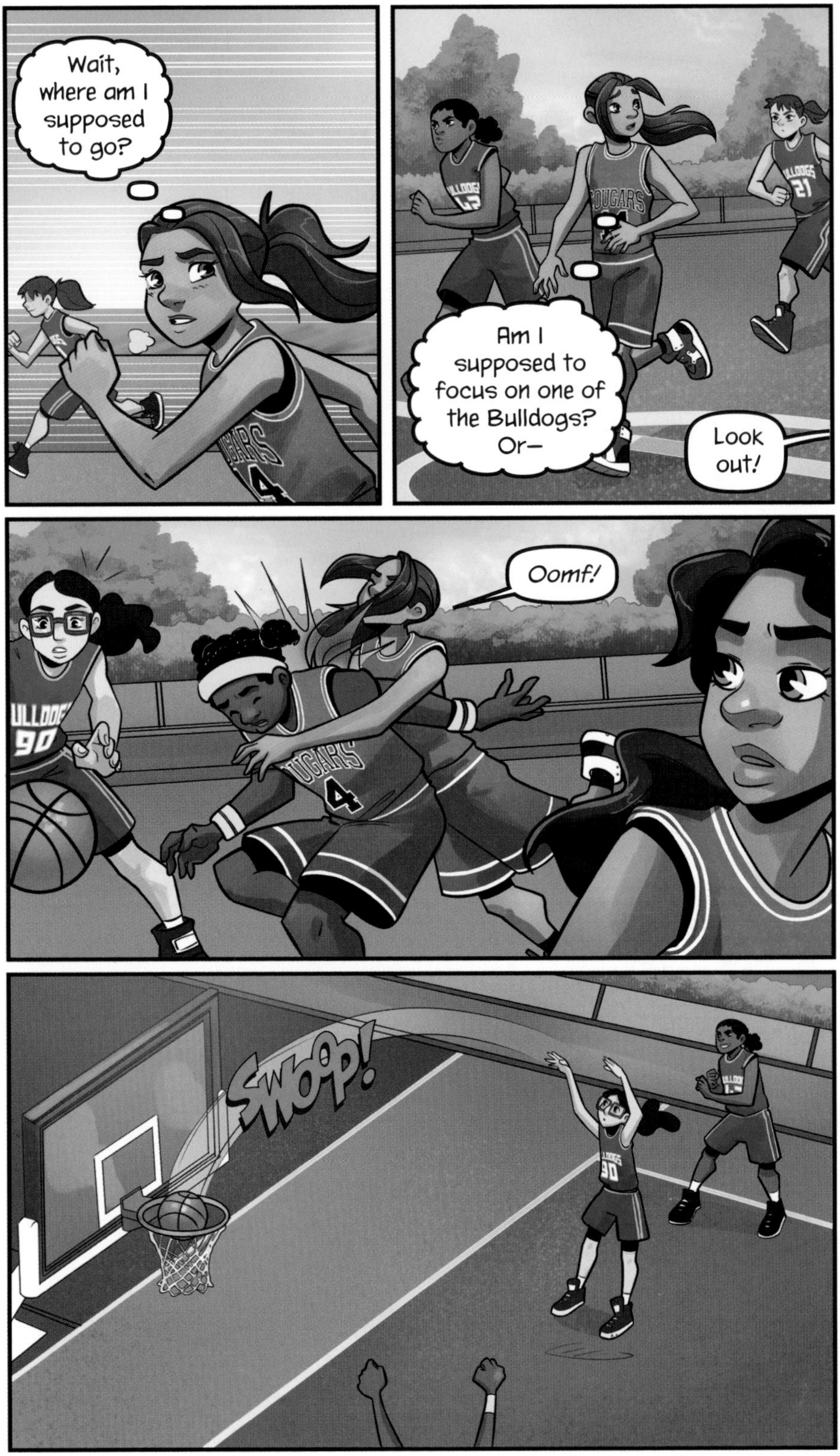
Wait, where am I supposed to go?
Am I supposed to focus on one of the Bulldogs? Or—
Look out!
Oomf!
SWOOP!

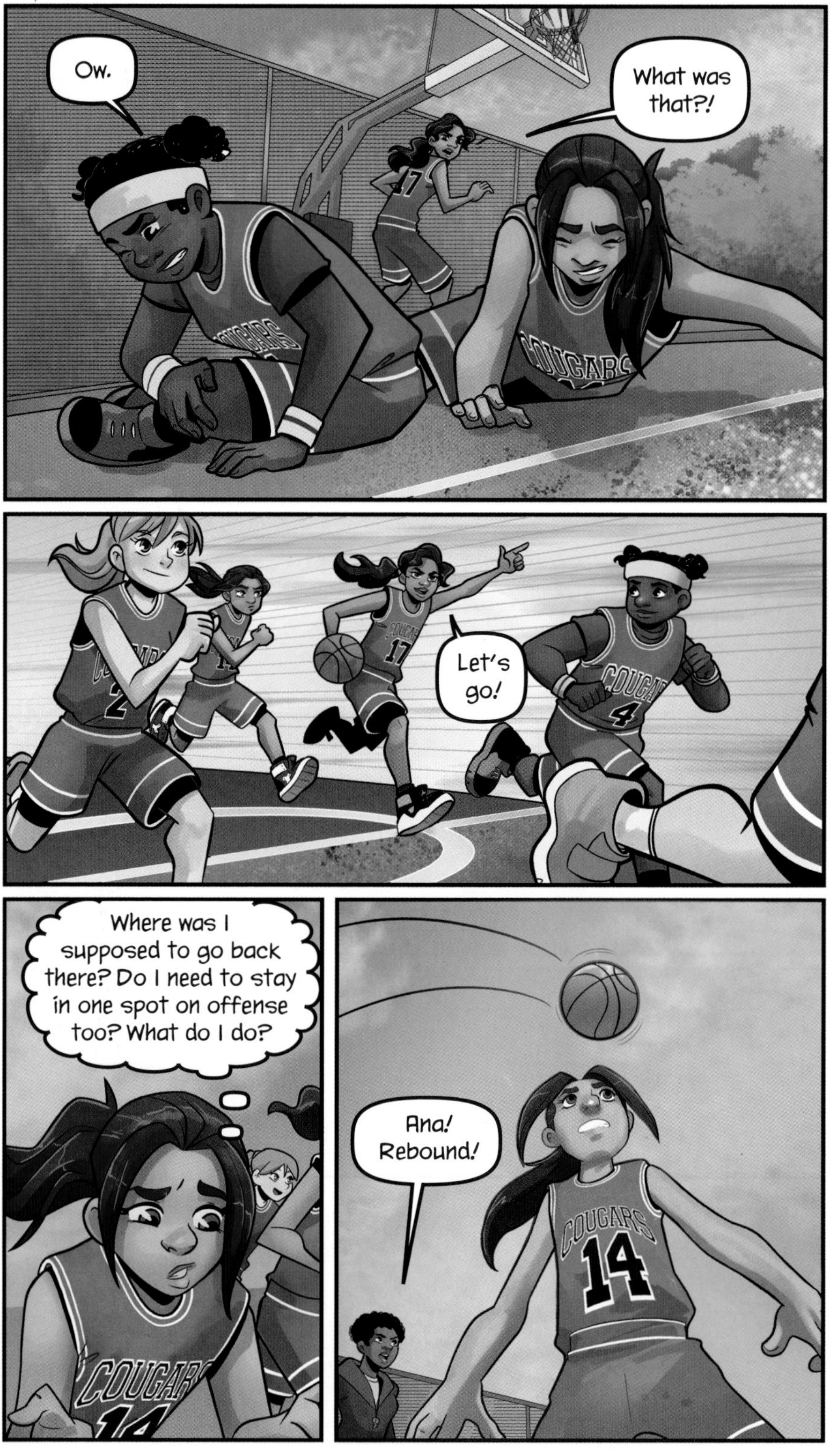
Ow.
What was that?!
Let's go!
Where was I supposed to go back there? Do I need to stay in one spot on offense too? What do I do?
Ana! Rebound!

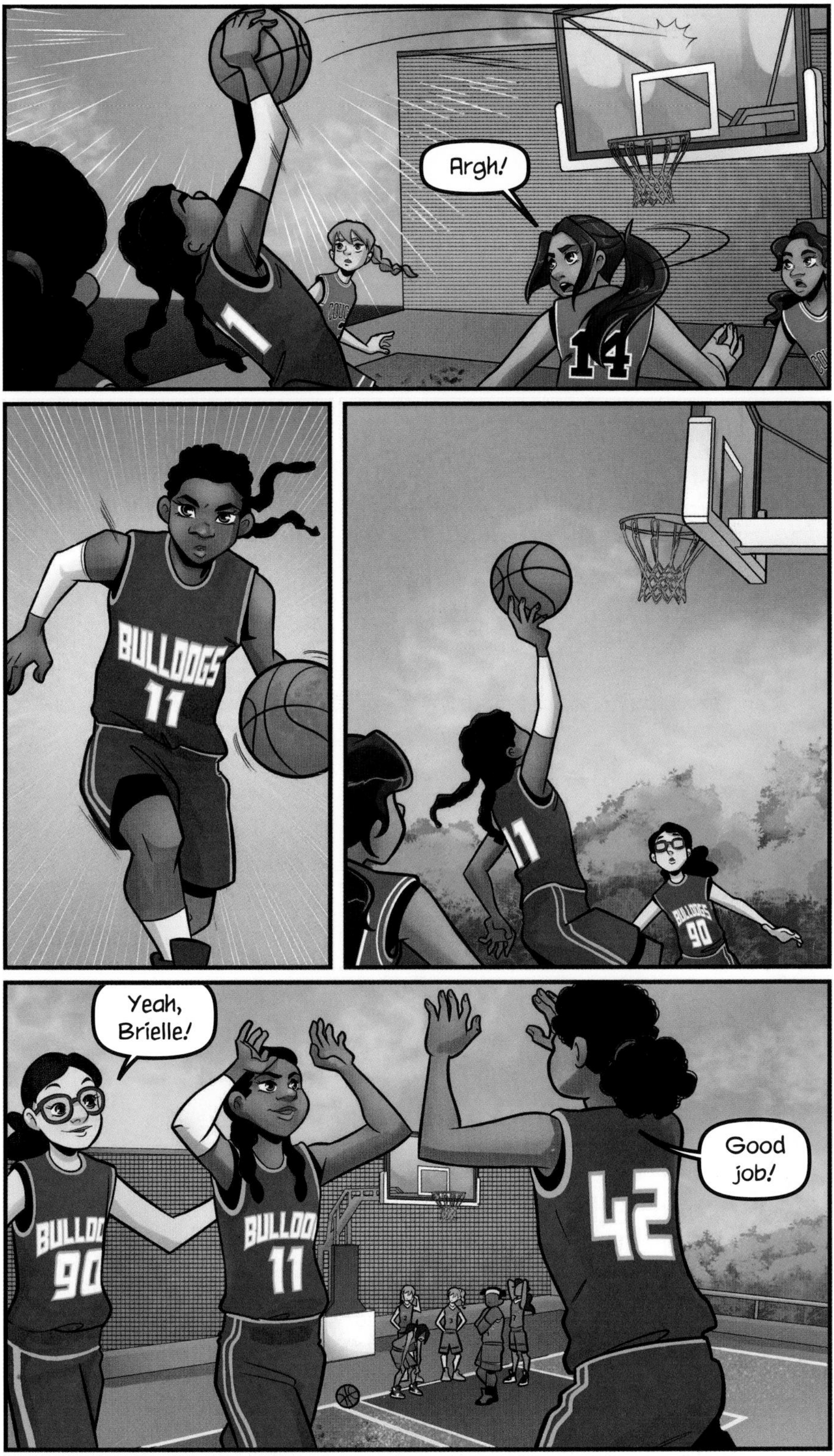
Argh!
Yeah, Brielle!
Good job!

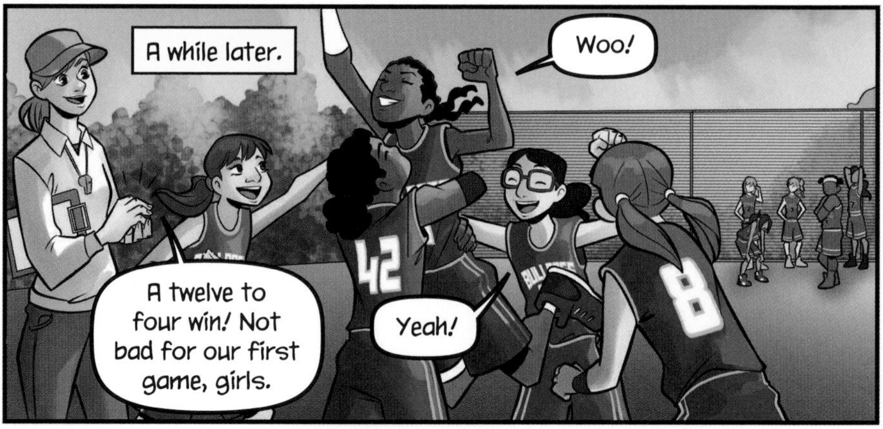
A while later.
Woo!
A twelve to four win! Not bad for our first game, girls.
Yeah!
42
8

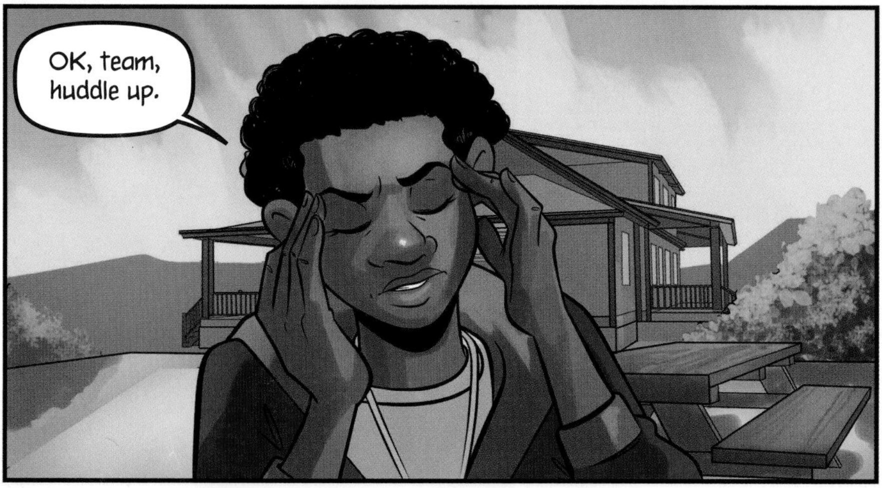
OK, team, huddle up.

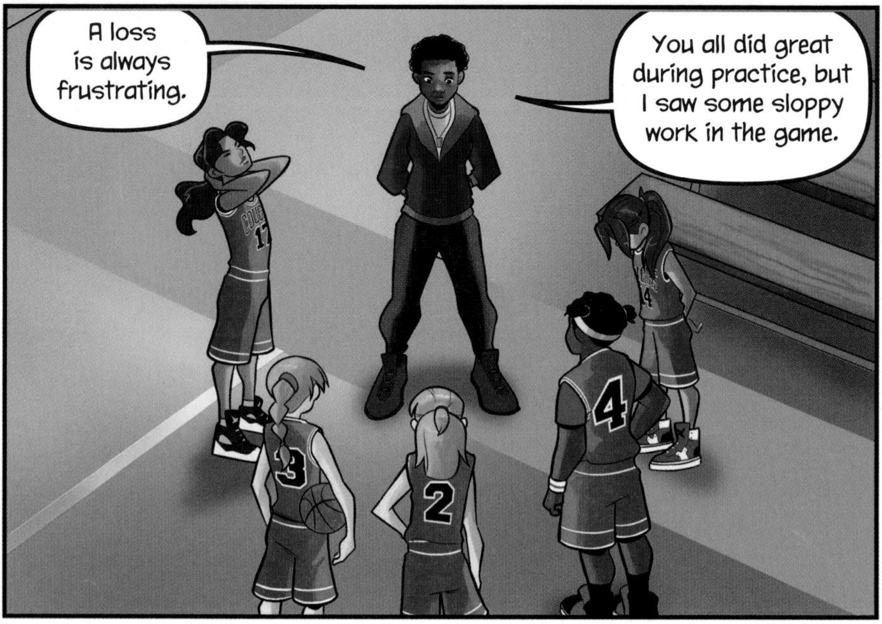
A loss is always frustrating.
You all did great during practice, but I saw some sloppy work in the game.

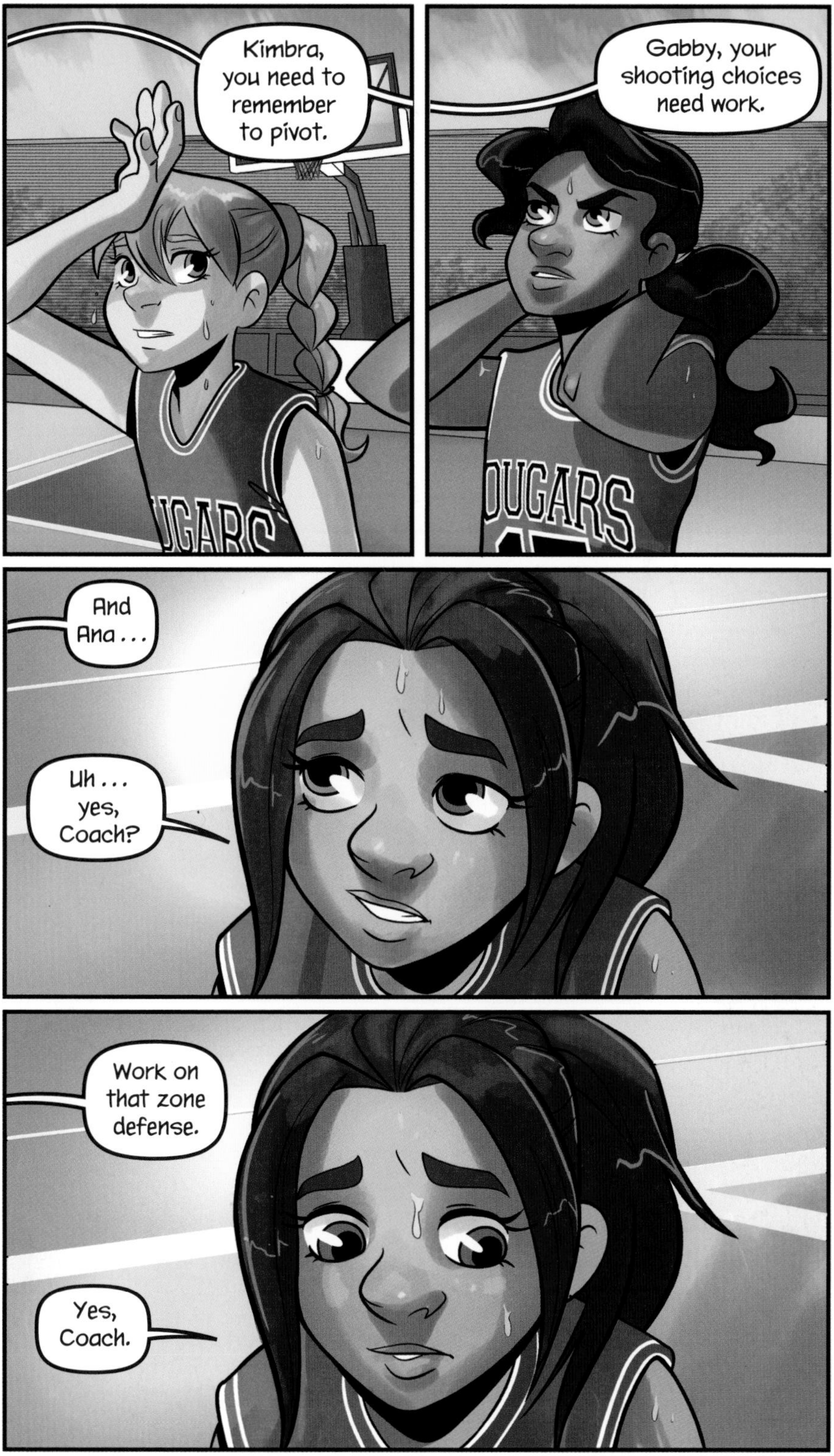
Kimbra, you need to remember to pivot.
Gabby, your shooting choices need work.
And Ana . . .
Uh . . . yes, Coach?
Work on that zone defense.
Yes, Coach.

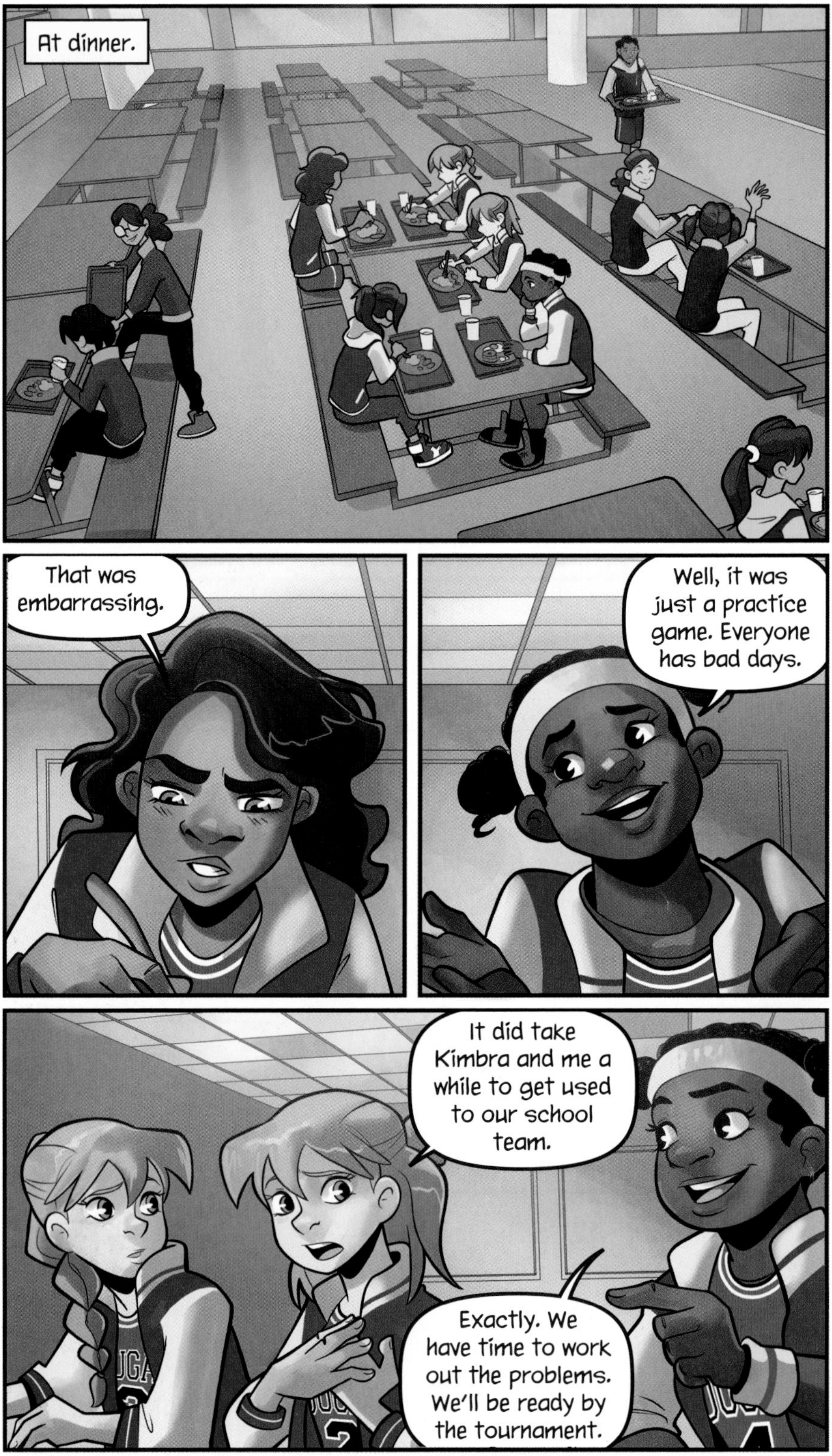
At dinner.
That was embarrassing.
Well, it was just a practice game. Everyone has bad days.
It did take Kimbra and me a while to get used to our school team.
Exactly. We have time to work out the problems. We'll be ready by the tournament.

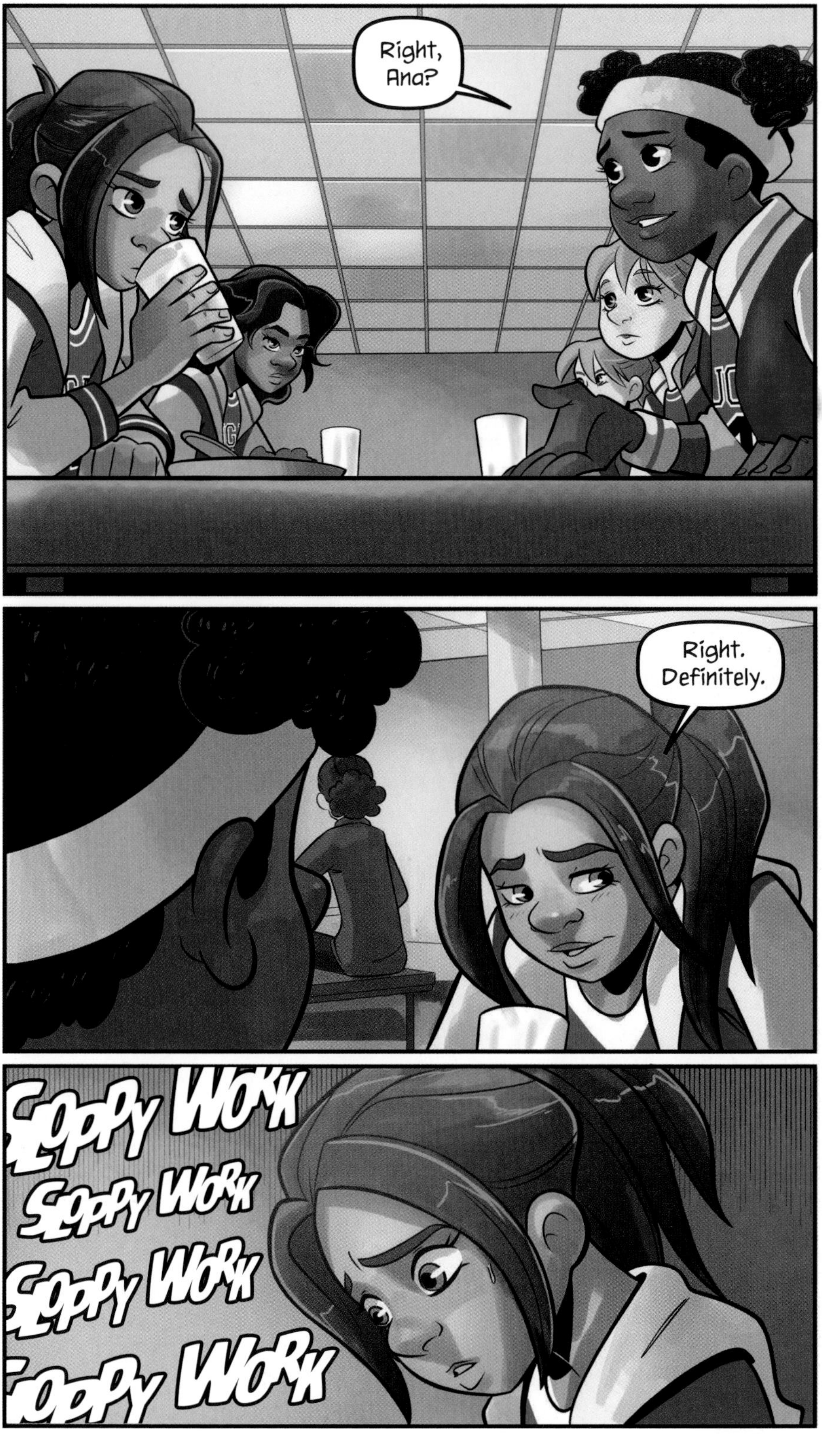
Right, Ana?
Right. Definitely.
SLOPPY WORK
SLOPPY WORK
SLOPPY WORK
SLOPPY WORK

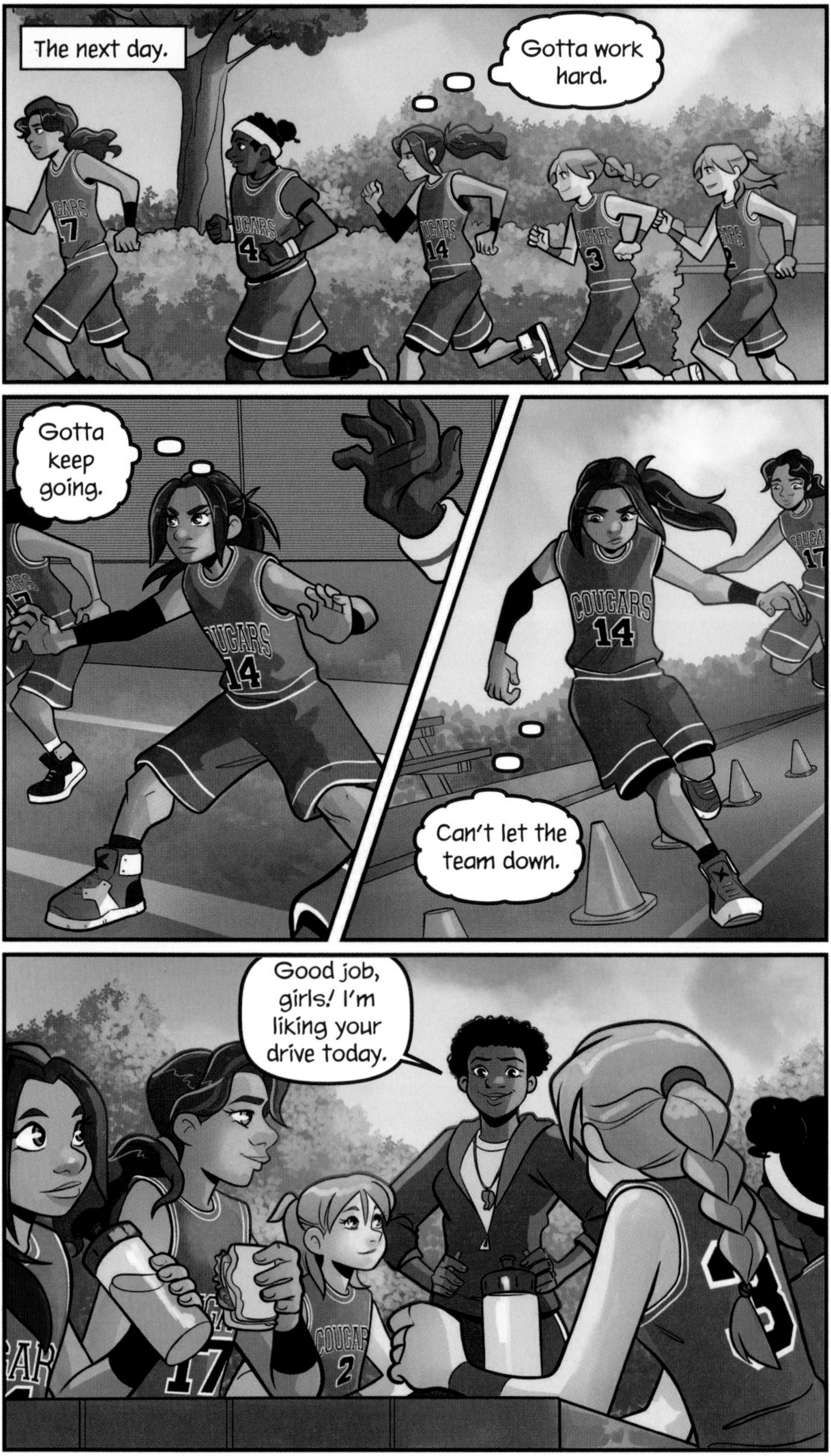
The next day.
Gotta work hard.
Gotta keep going.
Can't let the team down.
Good job, girls! I'm liking your drive today.

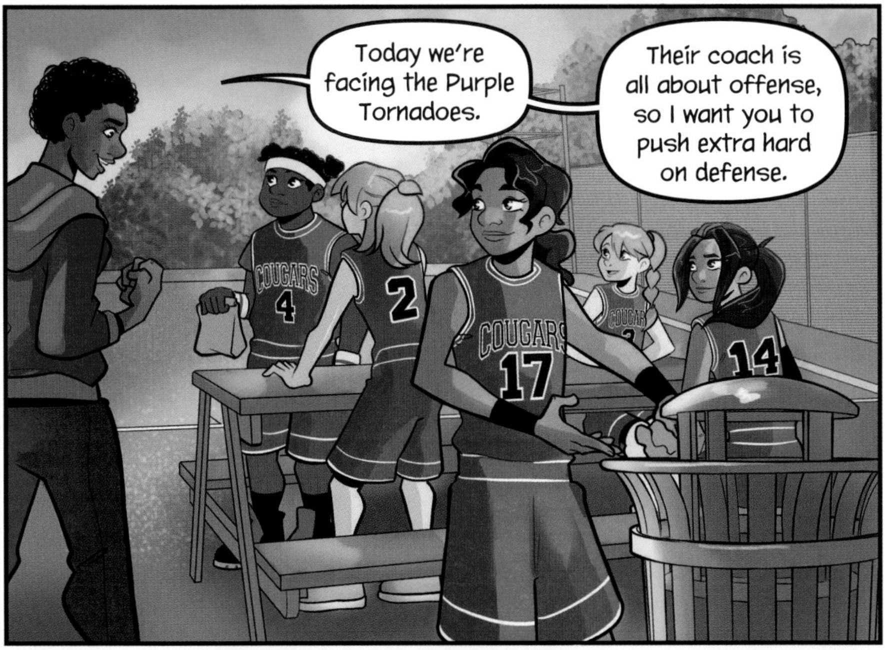
Today we're facing the Purple Tornadoes.
Their coach is all about offense, so I want you to push extra hard on defense.
COUGARS 4
2
COUGARS 17
14

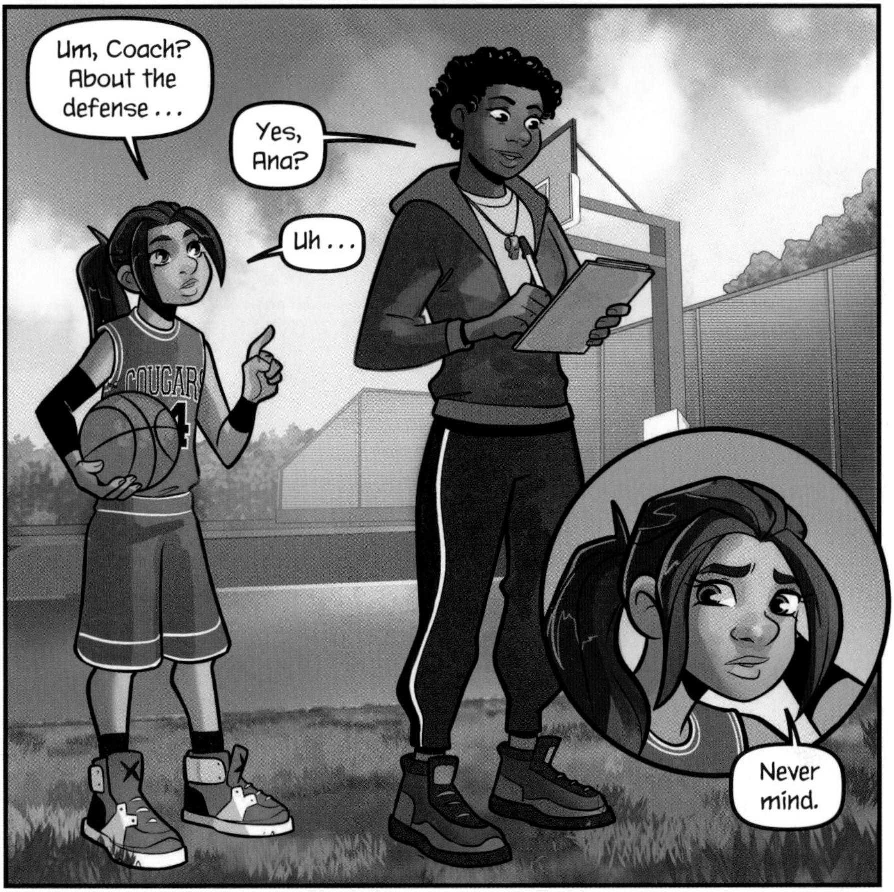
Um, Coach? About the defense . . .
Yes, Ana?
Uh . . .
COUGARS
Never mind.

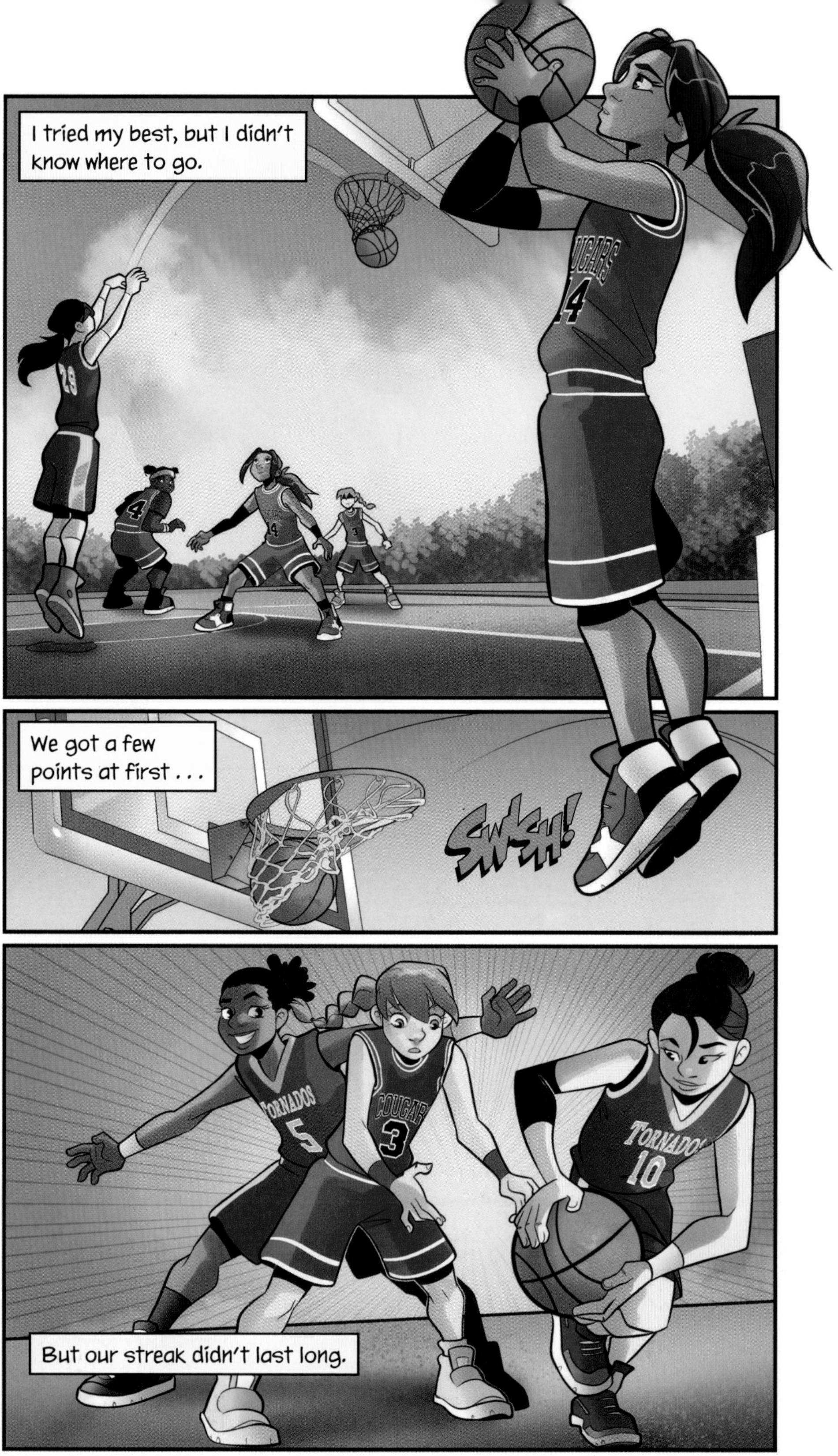
I tried my best, but I didn't know where to go.
COUGARS 14
29
4
COUGARS 14
3
We got a few points at first . . .
SWISH!
TORNADOS 5
COUGAR 3
TORNADOS 10
But our streak didn't last long.

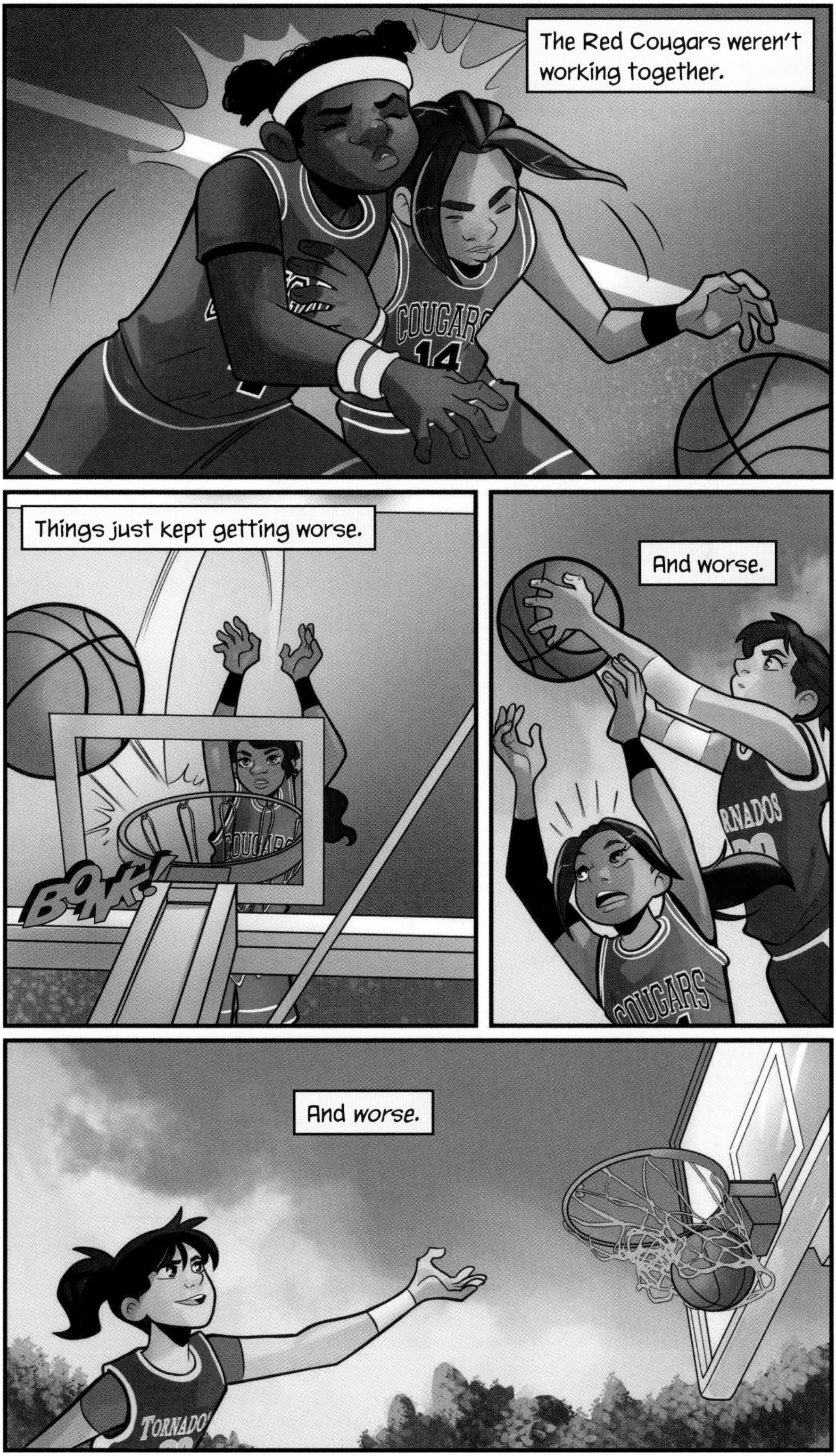
The Red Cougars weren't working together.
COUGARS
14
Things just kept getting worse.
BONK!
And worse.
And *worse*.

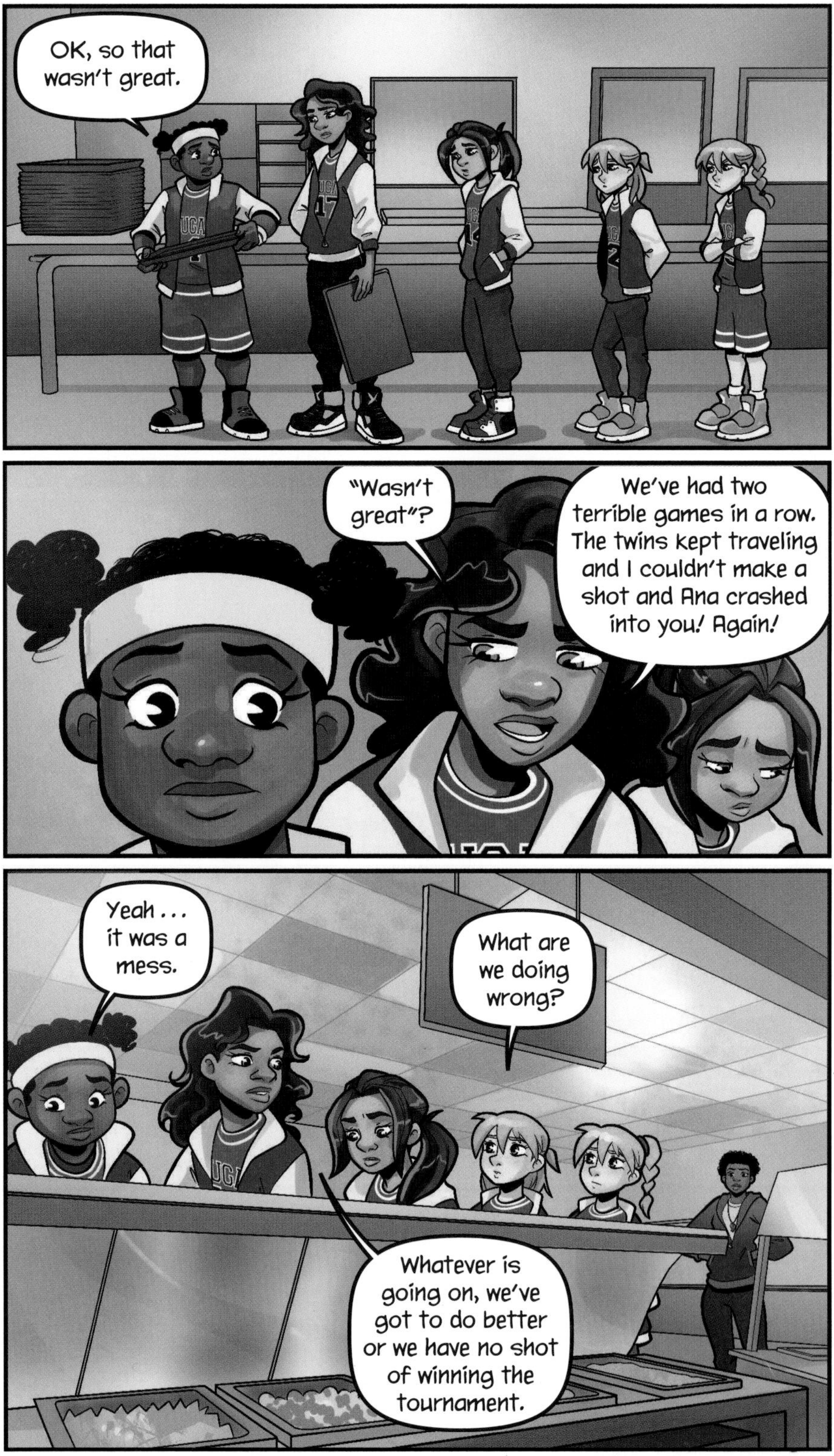
OK, so that wasn't great.
"Wasn't great"?
We've had two terrible games in a row. The twins kept traveling and I couldn't make a shot and Ana crashed into you! Again!
Yeah . . . it was a mess.
What are we doing wrong?
Whatever is going on, we've got to do better or we have no shot of winning the tournament.

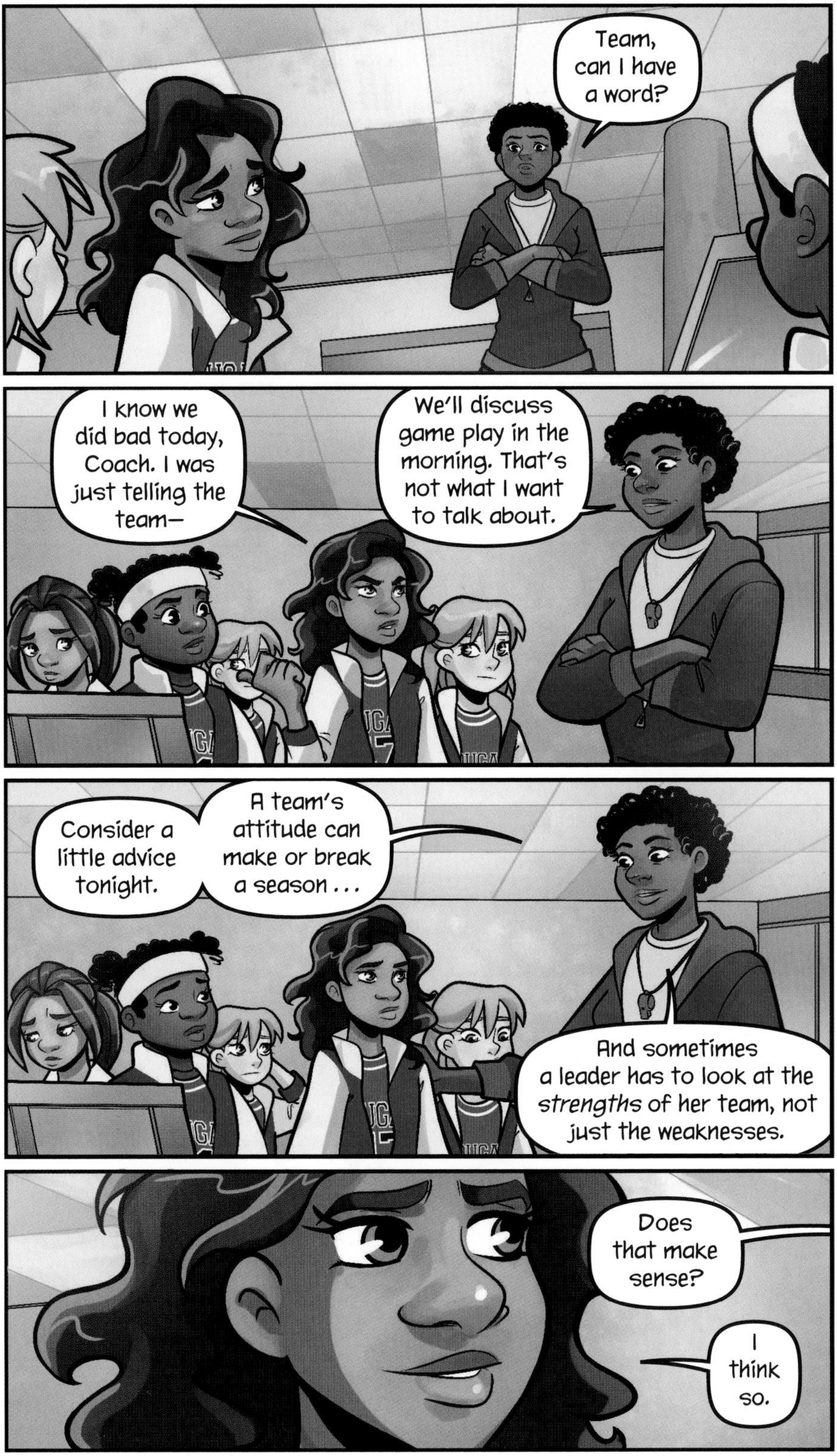
Team, can I have a word?
I know we did bad today, Coach. I was just telling the team—
We'll discuss game play in the morning. That's not what I want to talk about.
Consider a little advice tonight.
A team's attitude can make or break a season . . .
And sometimes a leader has to look at the *strengths* of her team, not just the weaknesses.
Does that make sense?
I think so.

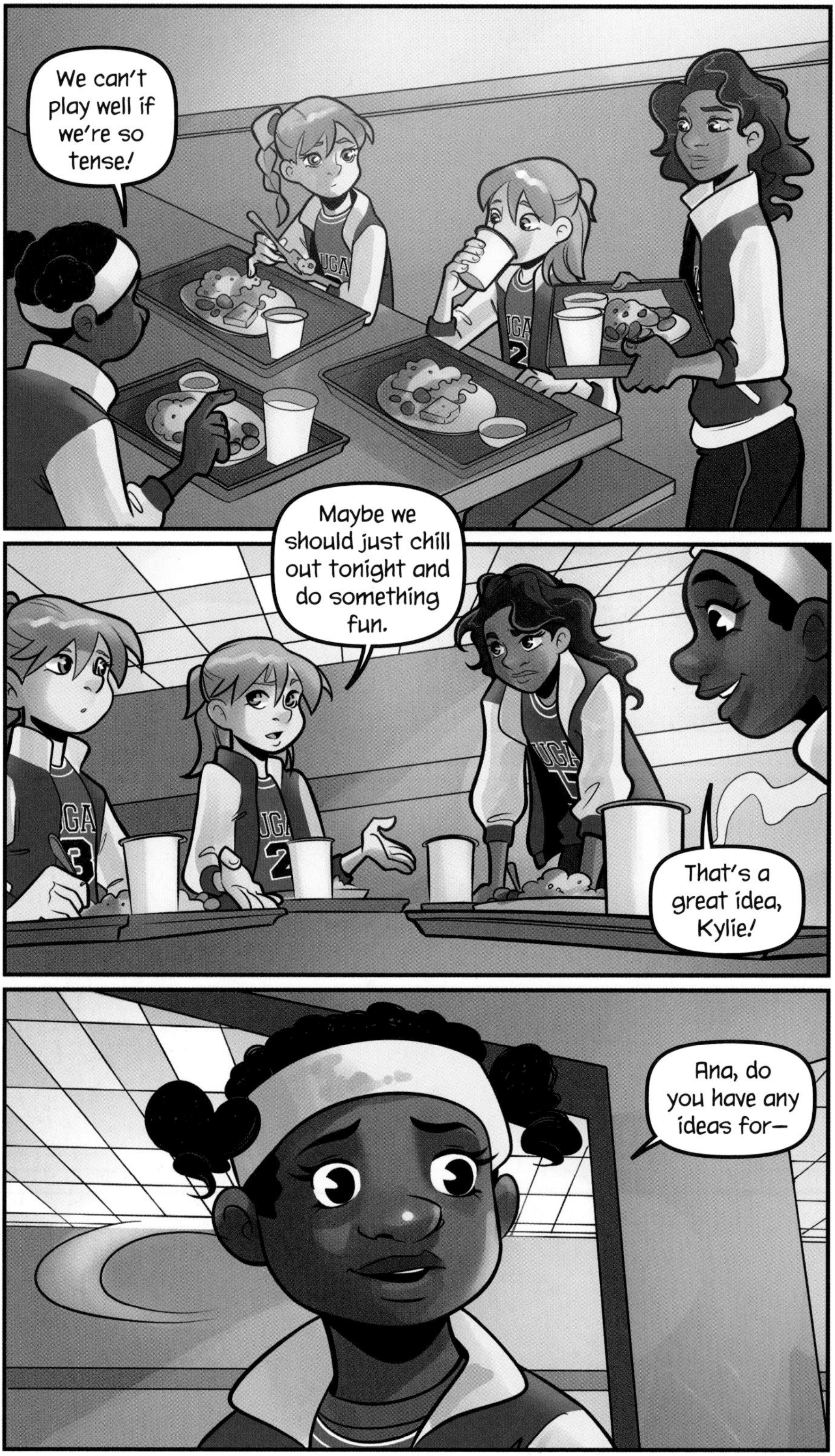
We can't play well if we're so tense!
Maybe we should just chill out tonight and do something fun.
That's a great idea, Kylie!
Ana, do you have any ideas for—

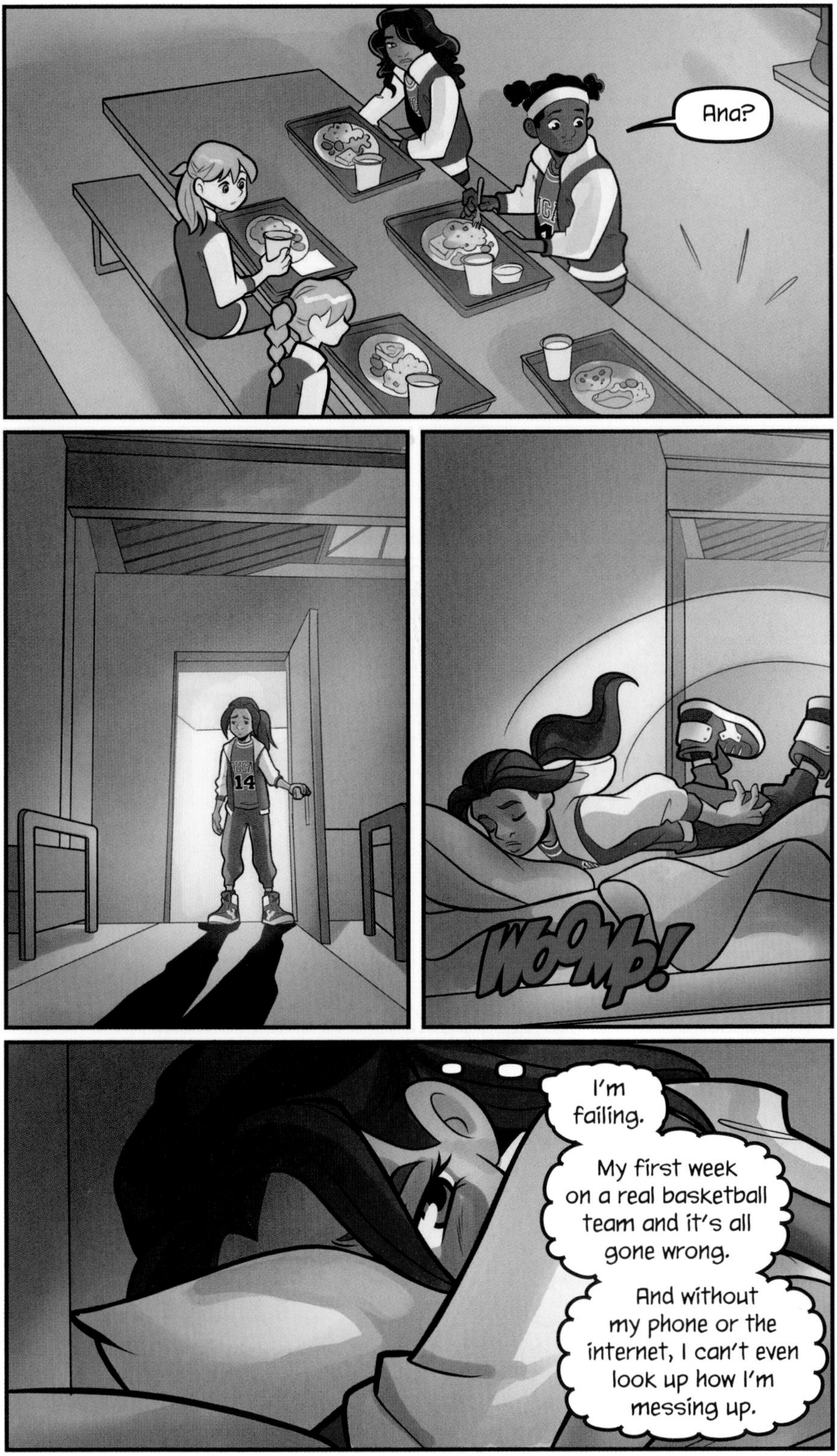

Ana?
WOOMP!
I'm failing.
My first week on a real basketball team and it's all gone wrong.
And without my phone or the internet, I can't even look up how I'm messing up.

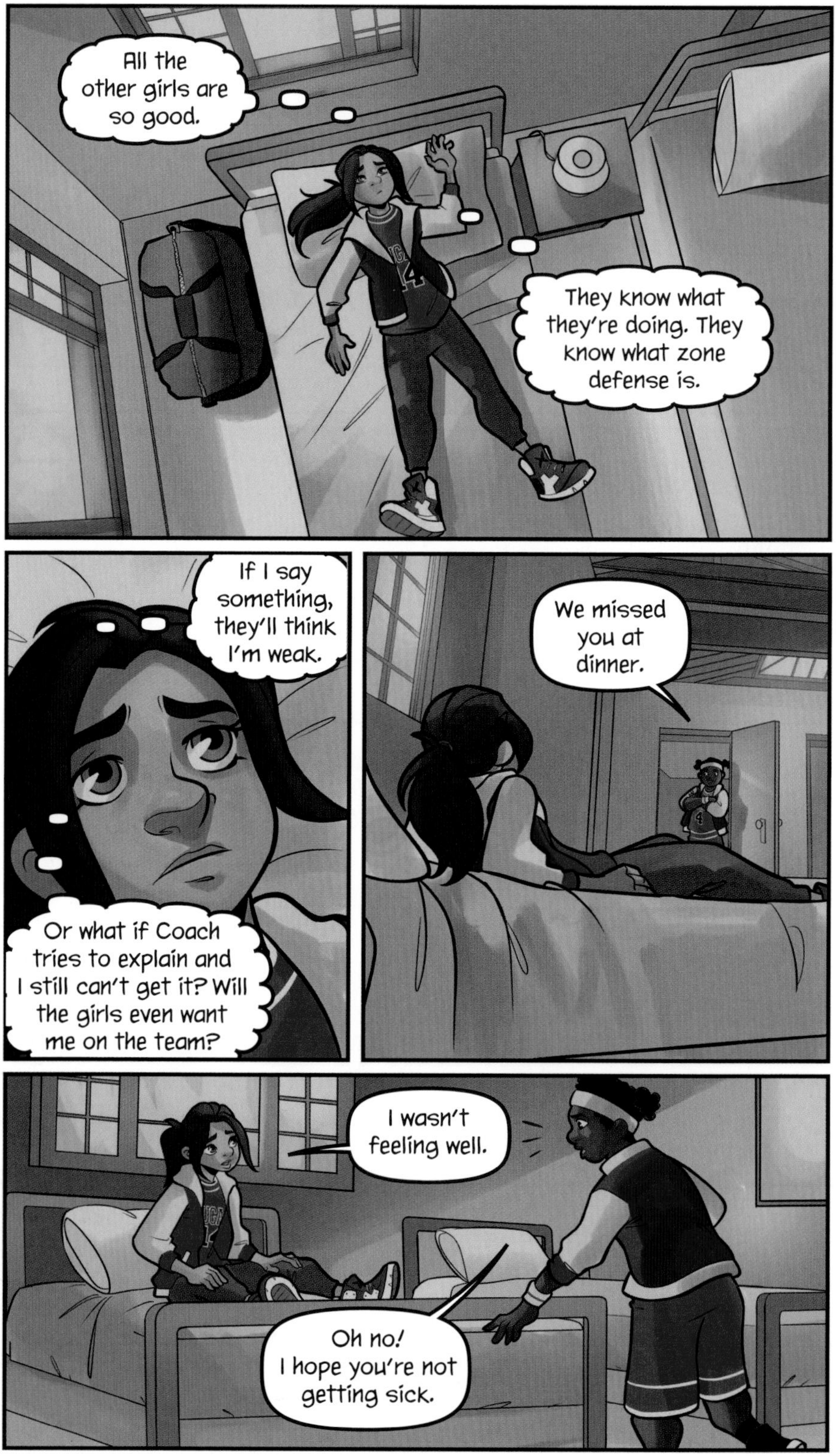
All the other girls are so good.
They know what they're doing. They know what zone defense is.
If I say something, they'll think I'm weak.
Or what if Coach tries to explain and I still can't get it? Will the girls even want me on the team?
We missed you at dinner.
I wasn't feeling well.
Oh no! I hope you're not getting sick.

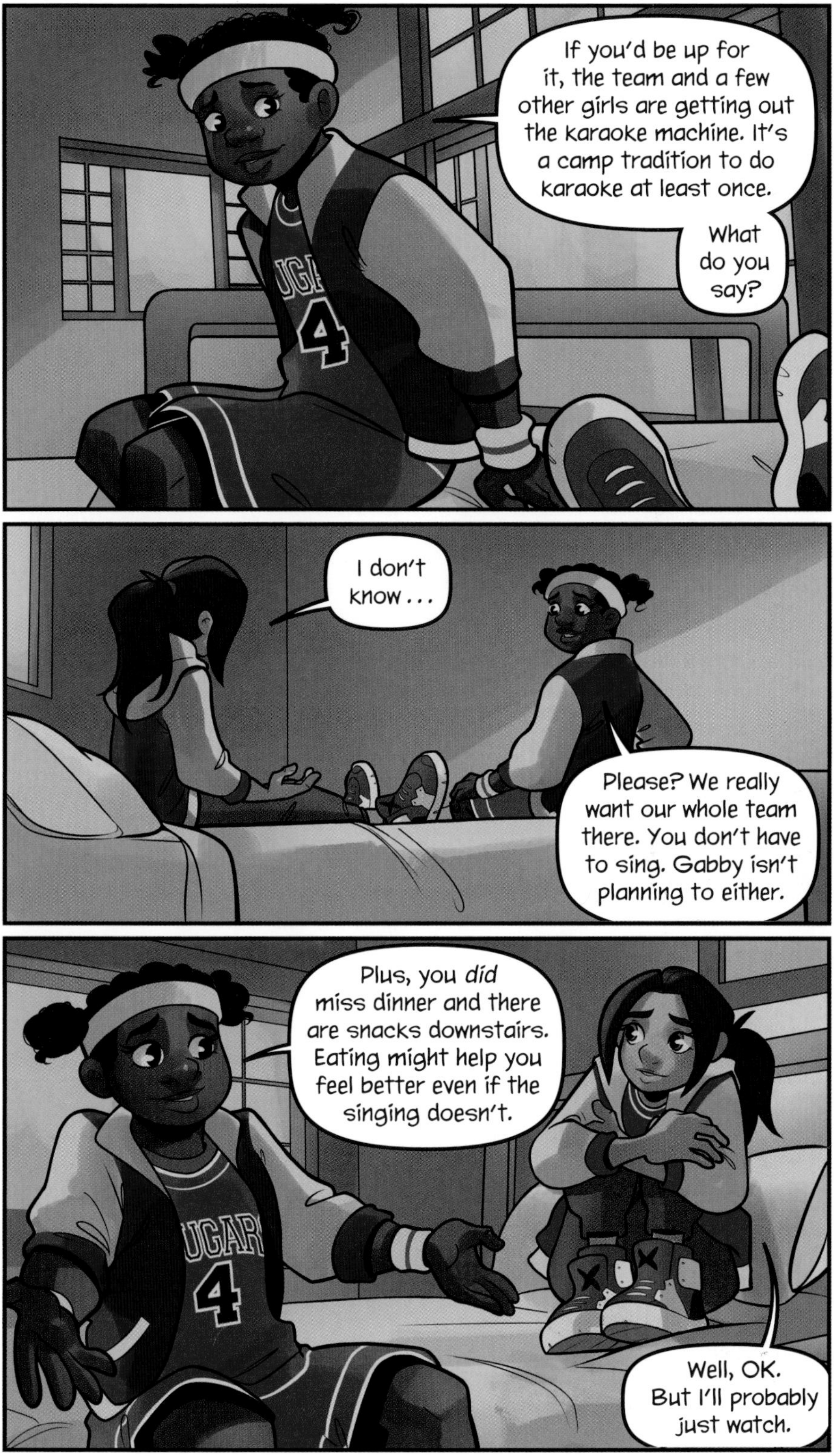
If you'd be up for it, the team and a few other girls are getting out the karaoke machine. It's a camp tradition to do karaoke at least once.
What do you say?
I don't know...
Please? We really want our whole team there. You don't have to sing. Gabby isn't planning to either.
Plus, you *did* miss dinner and there are snacks downstairs. Eating might help you feel better even if the singing doesn't.
Well, OK. But I'll probably just watch.

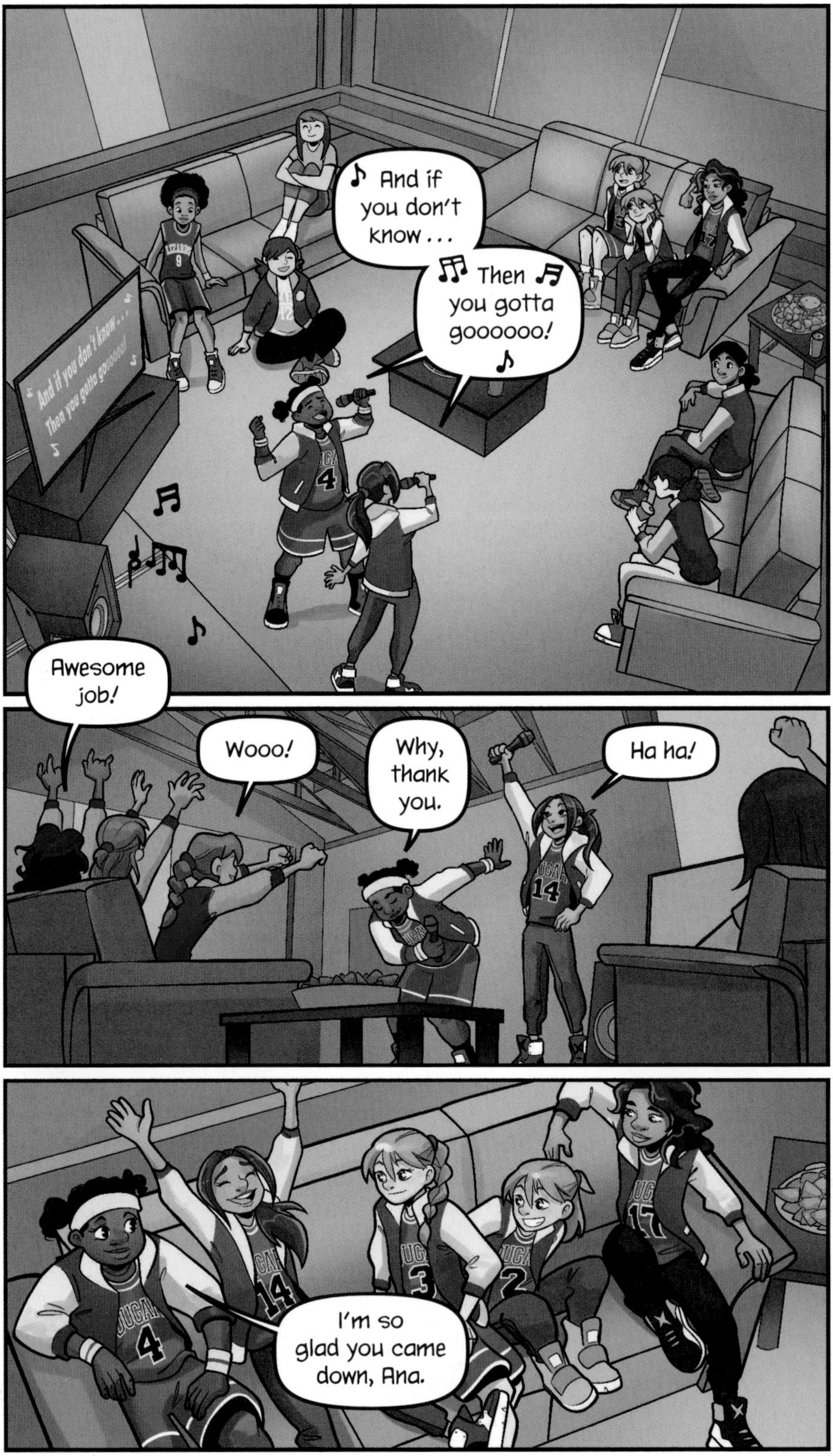
And if you don't know...
Then you gotta goooooo!
♪ And if you don't know . . .
♫ Then ♬ you gotta goooooo! ♪
Awesome job!
Wooo!
Why, thank you.
Ha ha!
I'm so glad you came down, Ana.

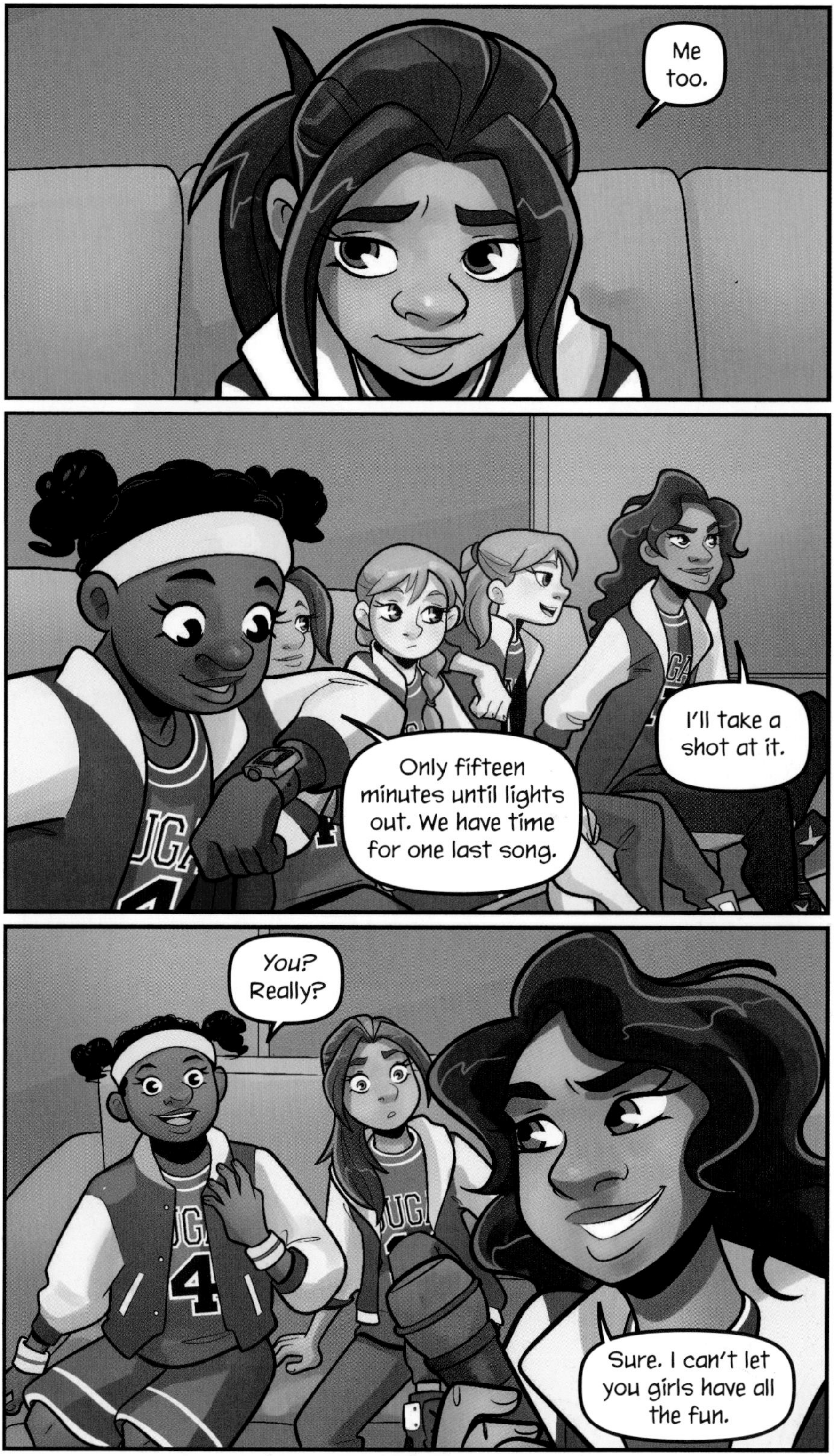
Me too.
Only fifteen minutes until lights out. We have time for one last song.
I'll take a shot at it.
You? Really?
Sure. I can't let you girls have all the fun.

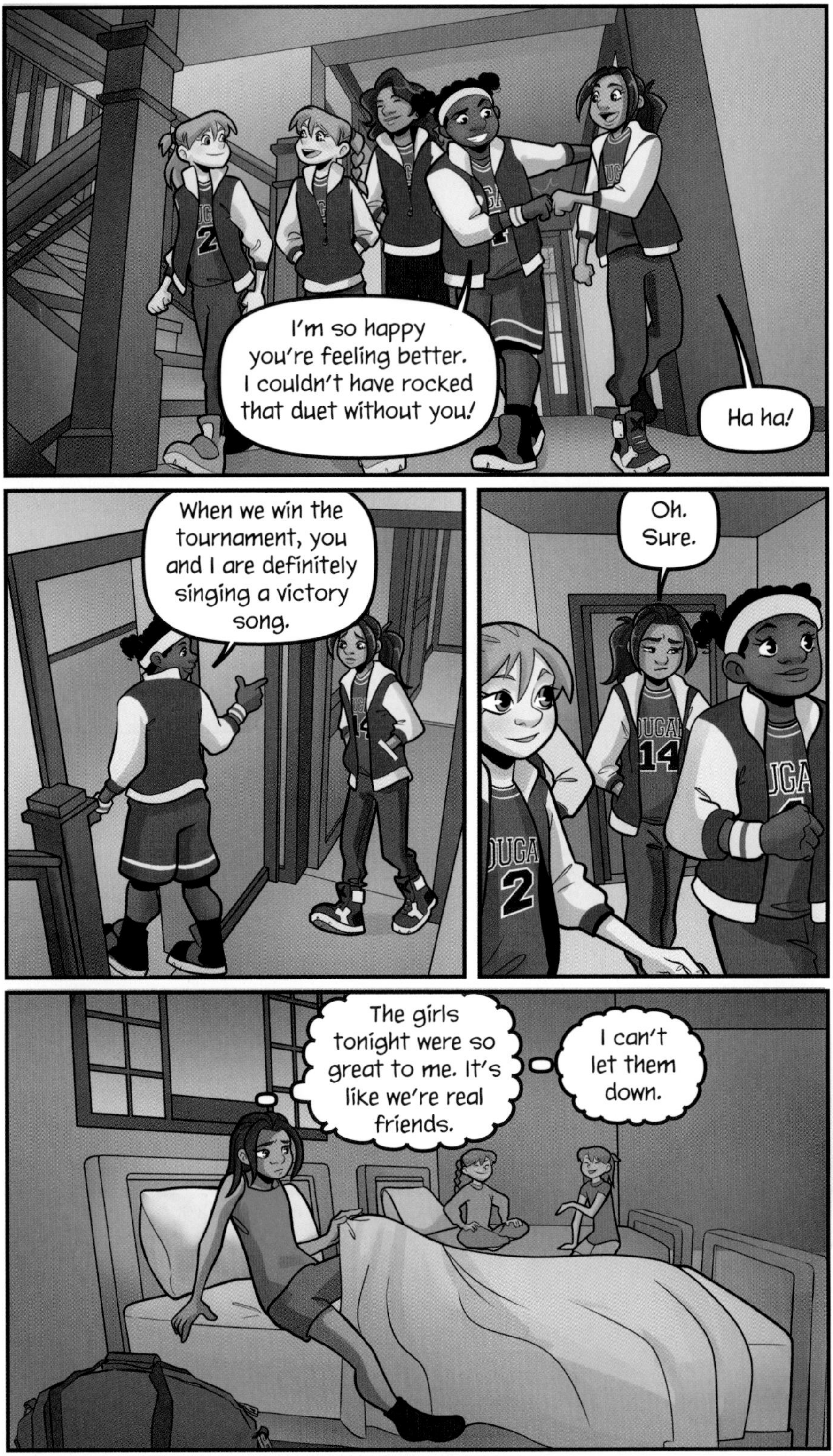
I'm so happy you're feeling better. I couldn't have rocked that duet without you!
Ha ha!
When we win the tournament, you and I are definitely singing a victory song.
Oh. Sure.
The girls tonight were so great to me. It's like we're real friends.
I can't let them down.

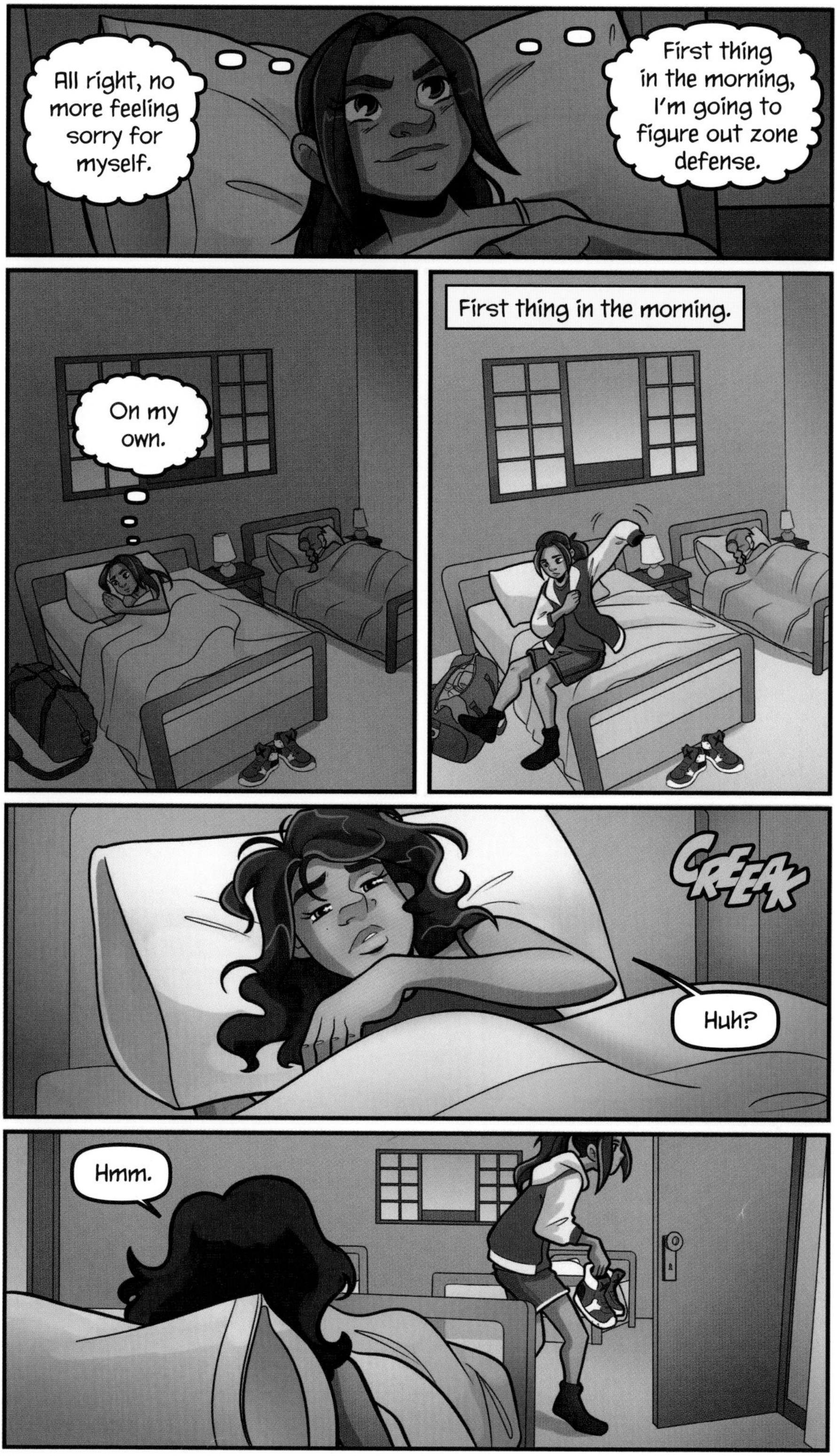
All right, no more feeling sorry for myself.
First thing in the morning, I'm going to figure out zone defense.
On my own.
First thing in the morning.
CREEAK
Huh?
Hmm.

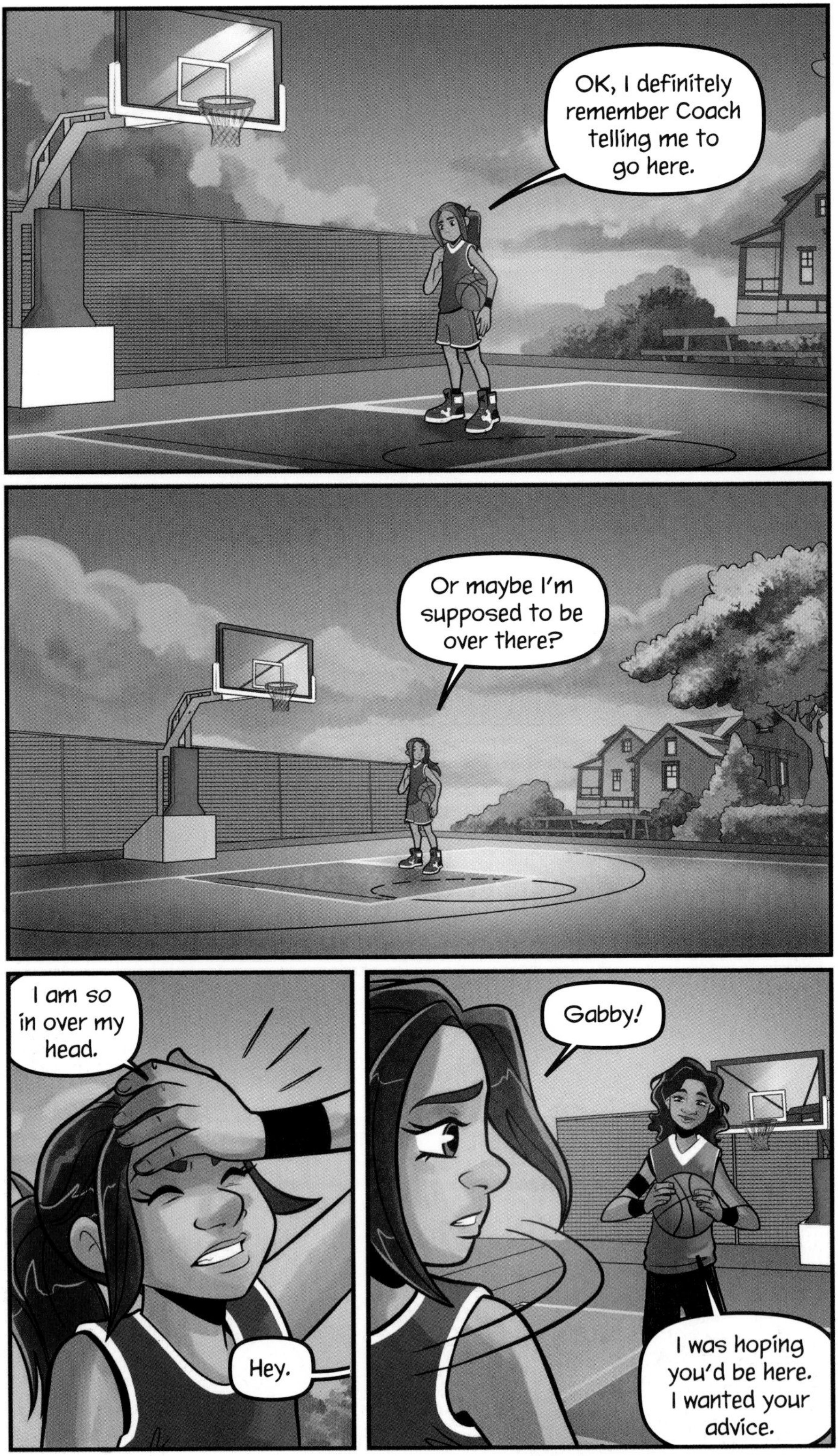
OK, I definitely remember Coach telling me to go here.
Or maybe I'm supposed to be over there?
I am so in over my head.
Hey.
Gabby!
I was hoping you'd be here. I wanted your advice.

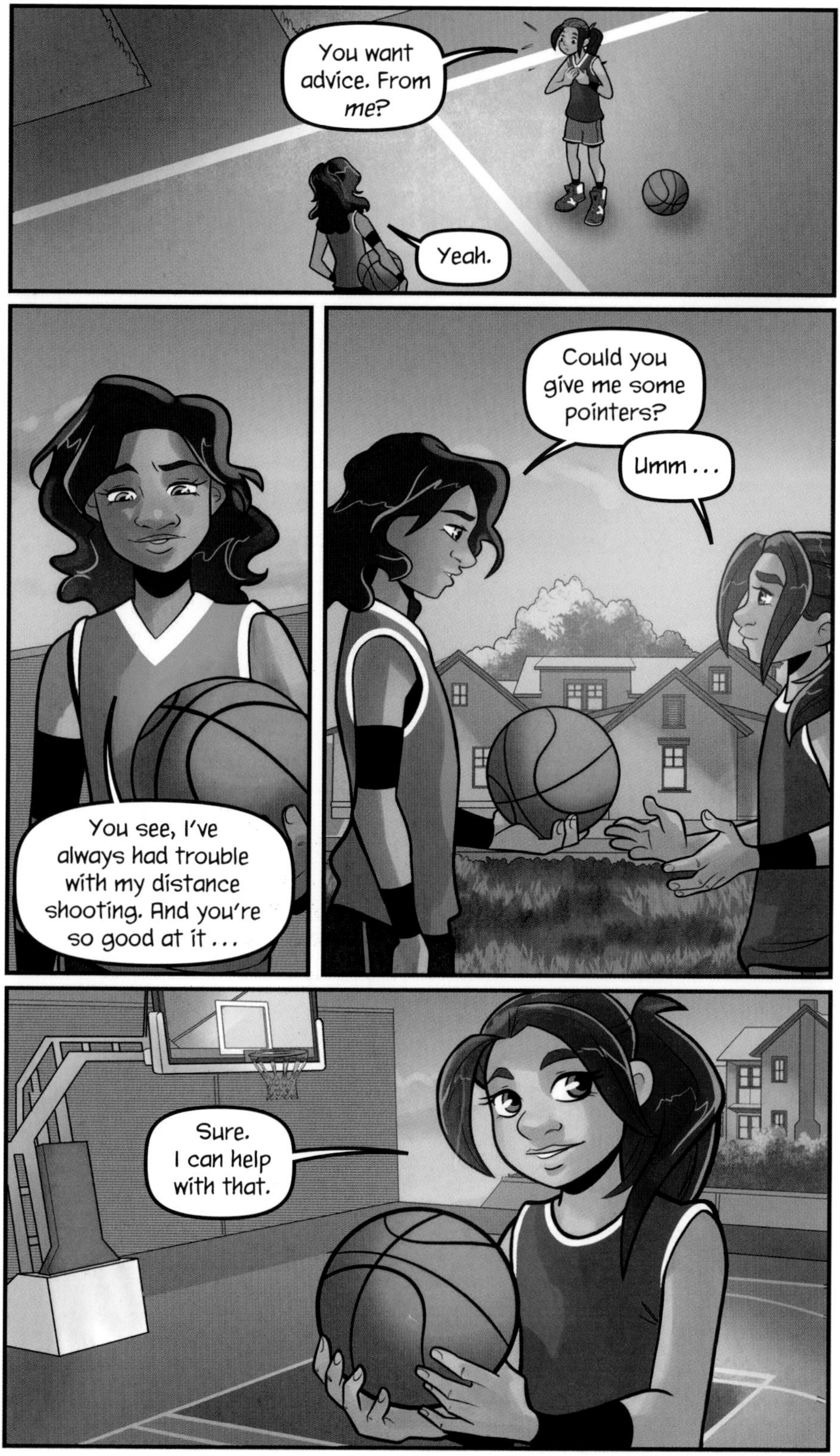
You want advice. From *me*?
Yeah.
You see, I've always had trouble with my distance shooting. And you're so good at it . . .
Could you give me some pointers?
Umm . . .
Sure. I can help with that.

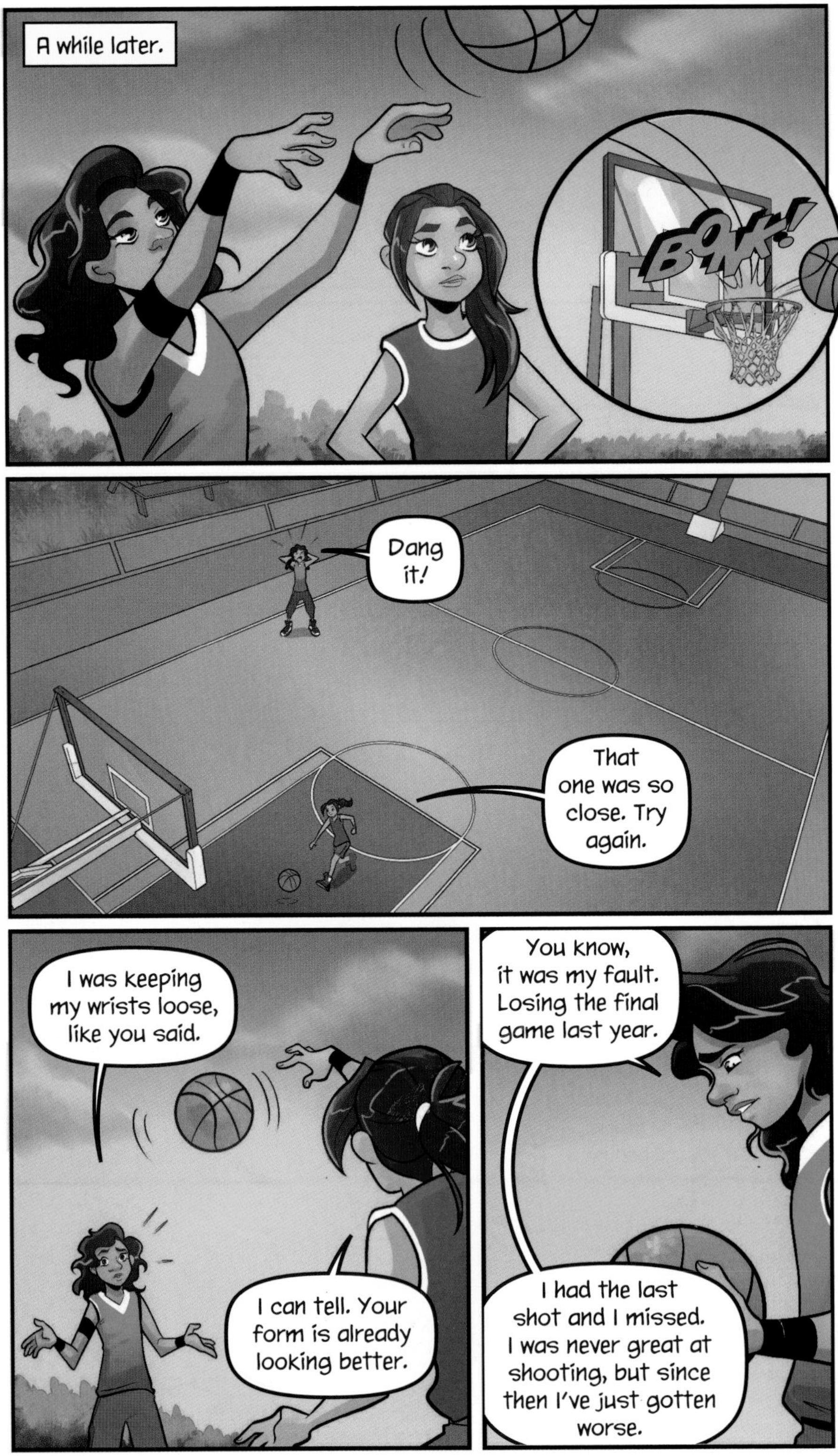
A while later.
BONK!
Dang it!
That one was so close. Try again.
I was keeping my wrists loose, like you said.
I can tell. Your form is already looking better.
You know, it was my fault. Losing the final game last year.
I had the last shot and I missed. I was never great at shooting, but since then I've just gotten worse.

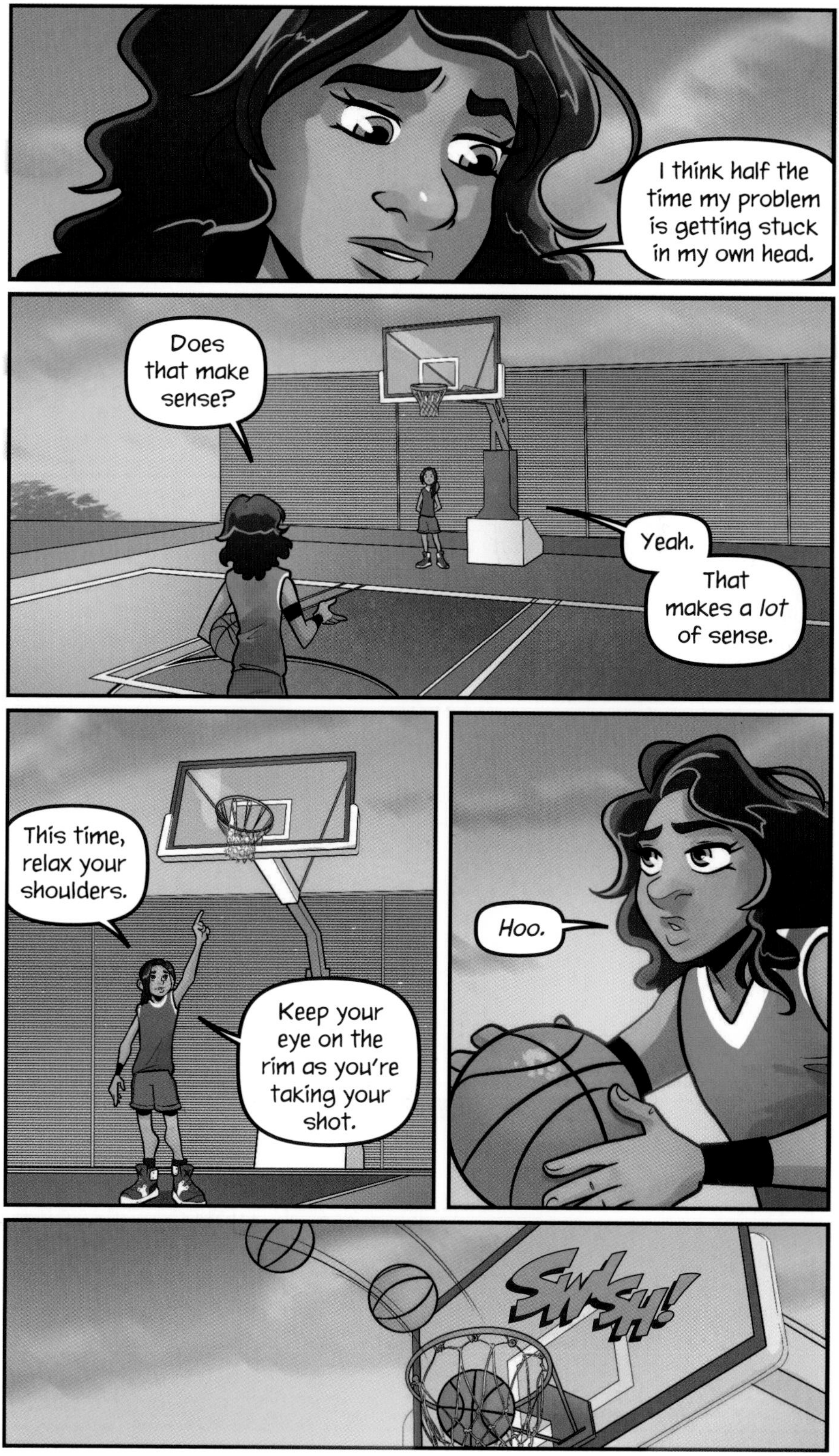
I think half the time my problem is getting stuck in my own head.
Does that make sense?
Yeah.
That makes a *lot* of sense.
This time, relax your shoulders.
Keep your eye on the rim as you're taking your shot.
Hoo.
SWISH!

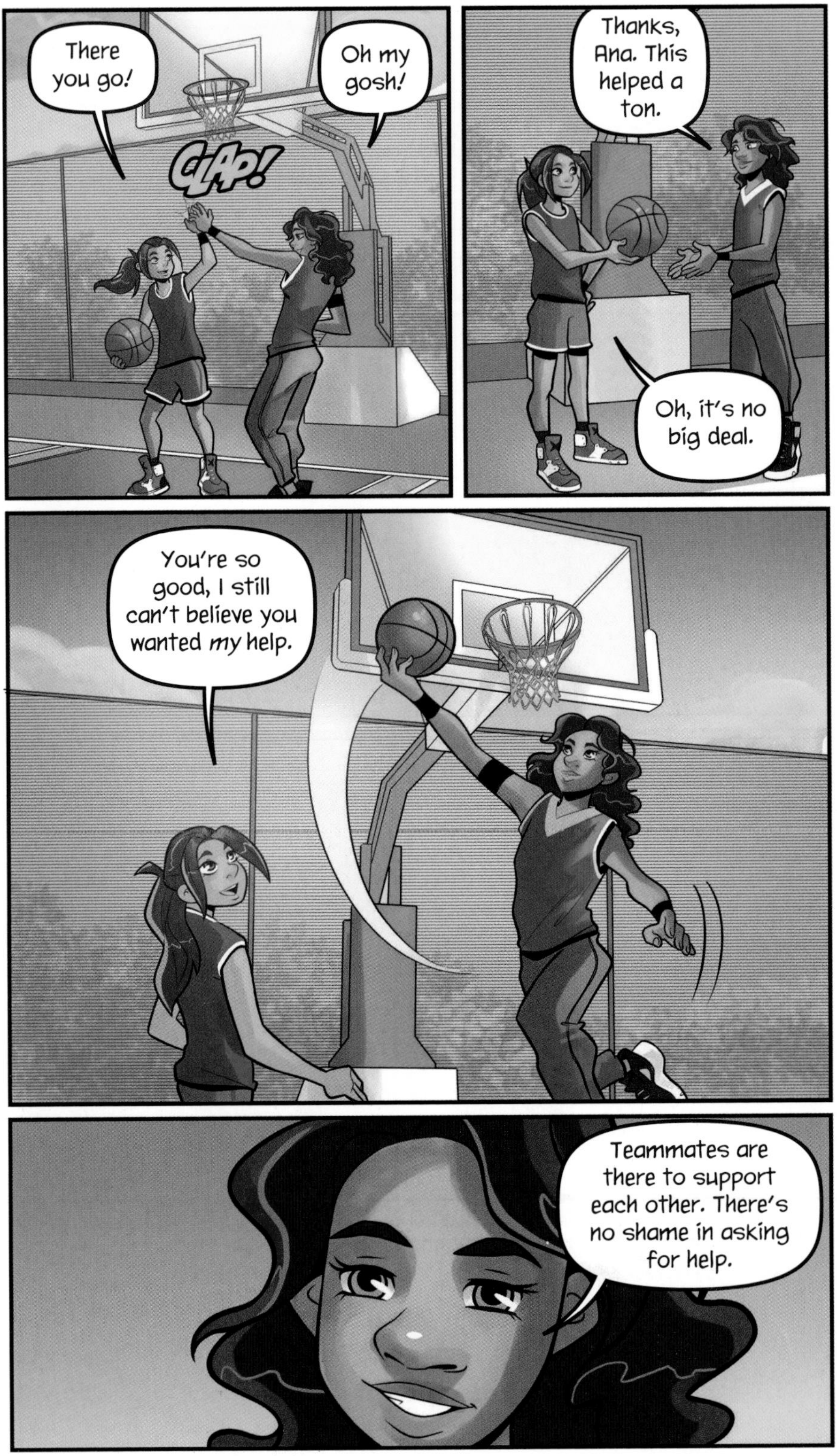
There you go!
Oh my gosh!
CLAP!
Thanks, Ana. This helped a ton.
Oh, it's no big deal.
You're so good, I still can't believe you wanted *my* help.
Teammates are there to support each other. There's no shame in asking for help.

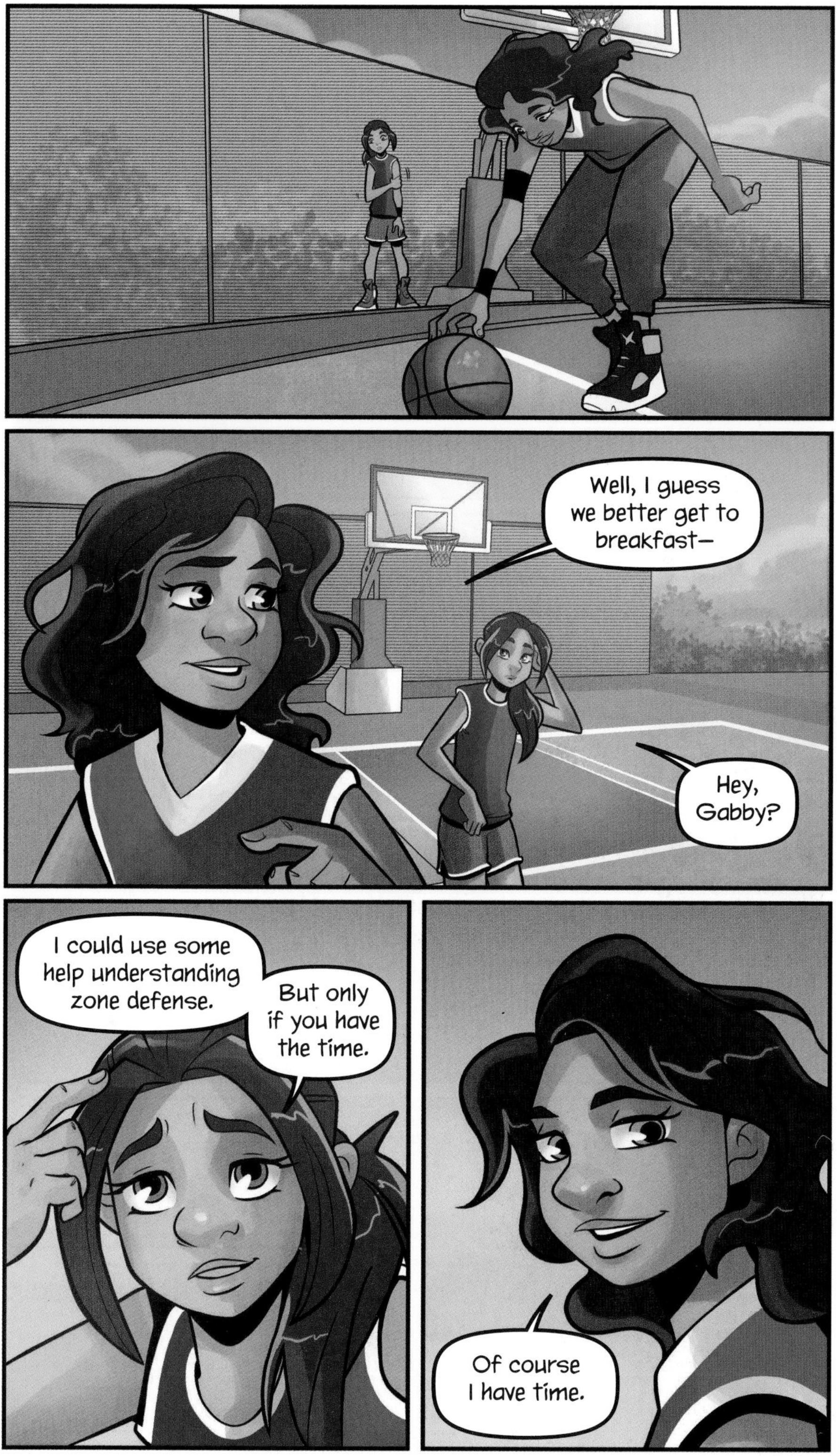
Well, I guess we better get to breakfast—
Hey, Gabby?
I could use some help understanding zone defense.
But only if you have the time.
Of course I have time.

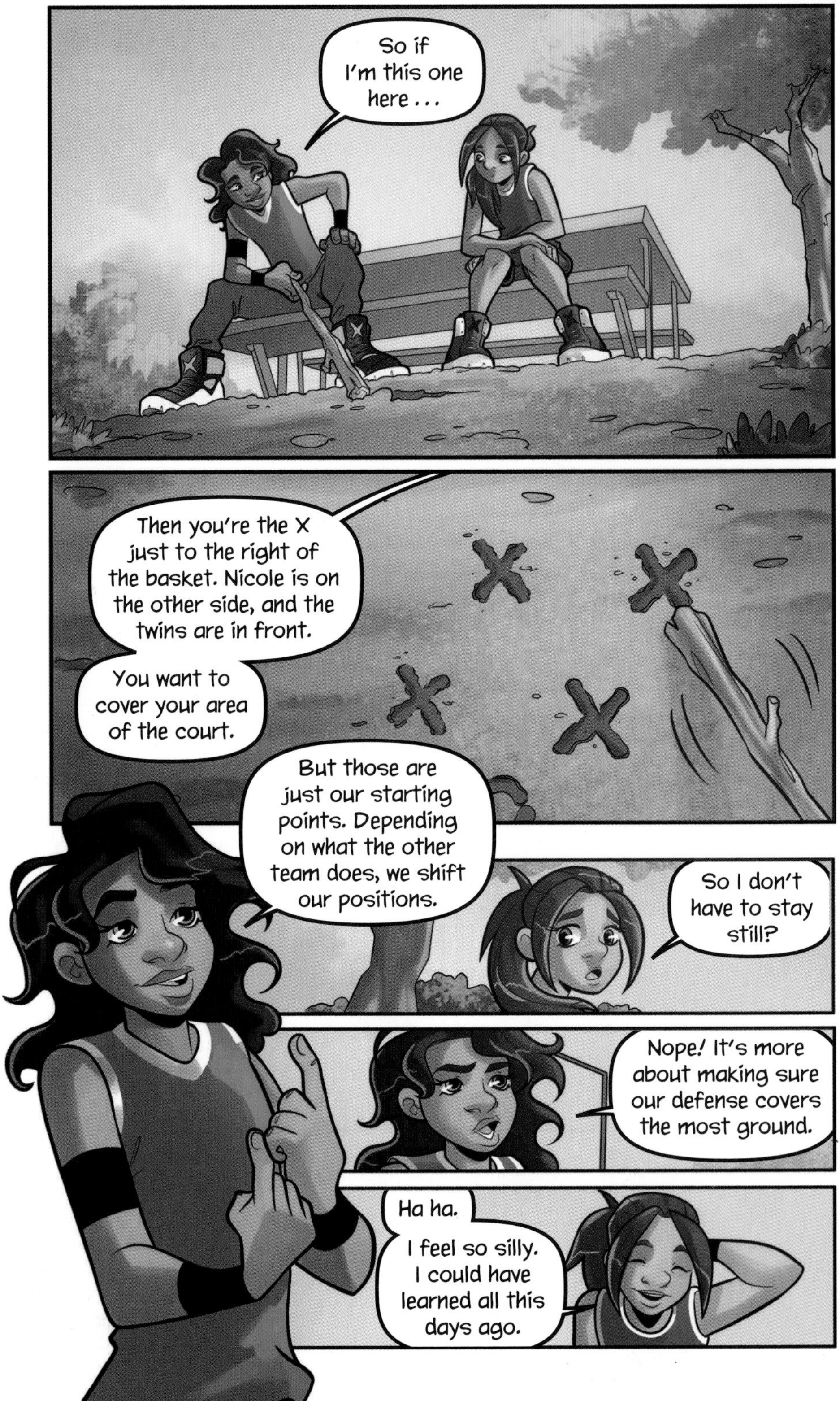
So if I'm this one here . . .
Then you're the X just to the right of the basket. Nicole is on the other side, and the twins are in front.
You want to cover your area of the court.
But those are just our starting points. Depending on what the other team does, we shift our positions.
So I don't have to stay still?
Nope! It's more about making sure our defense covers the most ground.
Ha ha.
I feel so silly. I could have learned all this days ago.

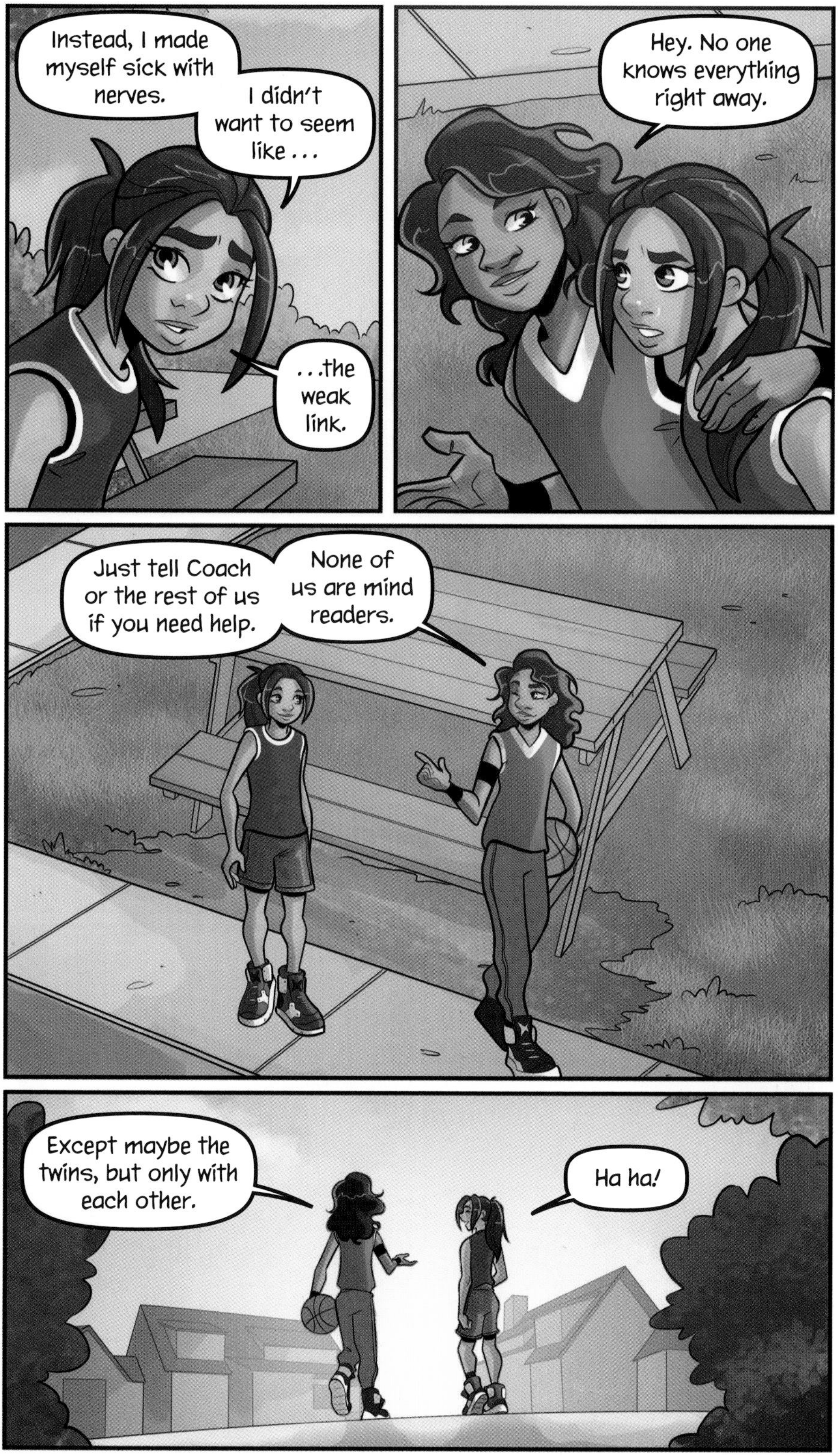

Instead, I made myself sick with nerves.
I didn't want to seem like . . .
. . .the weak link.
Hey. No one knows everything right away.
Just tell Coach or the rest of us if you need help.
None of us are mind readers.
Except maybe the twins, but only with each other.
Ha ha!

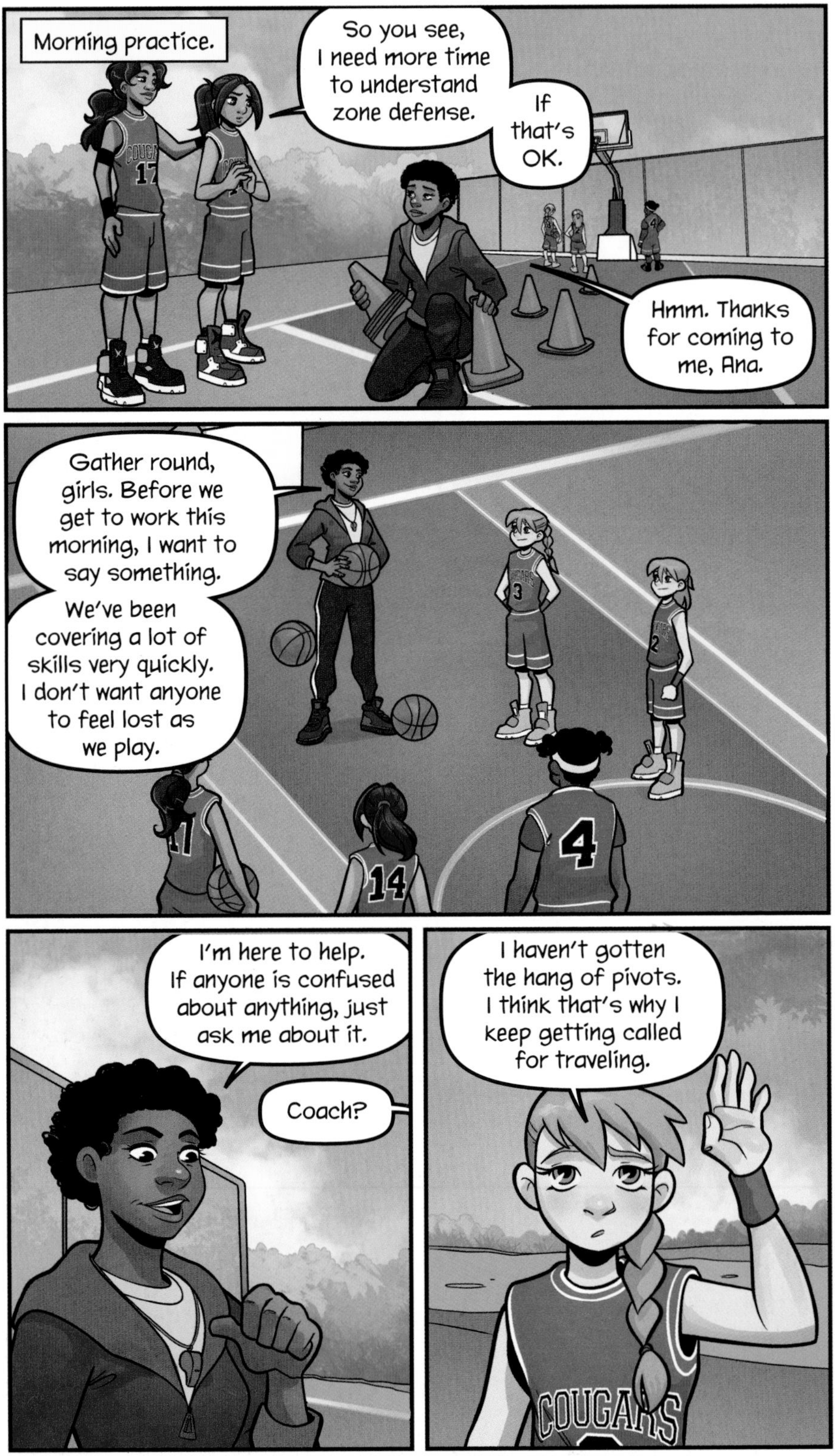
Morning practice.
So you see, I need more time to understand zone defense.
If that's OK.
Hmm. Thanks for coming to me, Ana.
Gather round, girls. Before we get to work this morning, I want to say something.
We've been covering a lot of skills very quickly. I don't want anyone to feel lost as we play.
I'm here to help. If anyone is confused about anything, just ask me about it.
Coach?
I haven't gotten the hang of pivots. I think that's why I keep getting called for traveling.
COUGARS

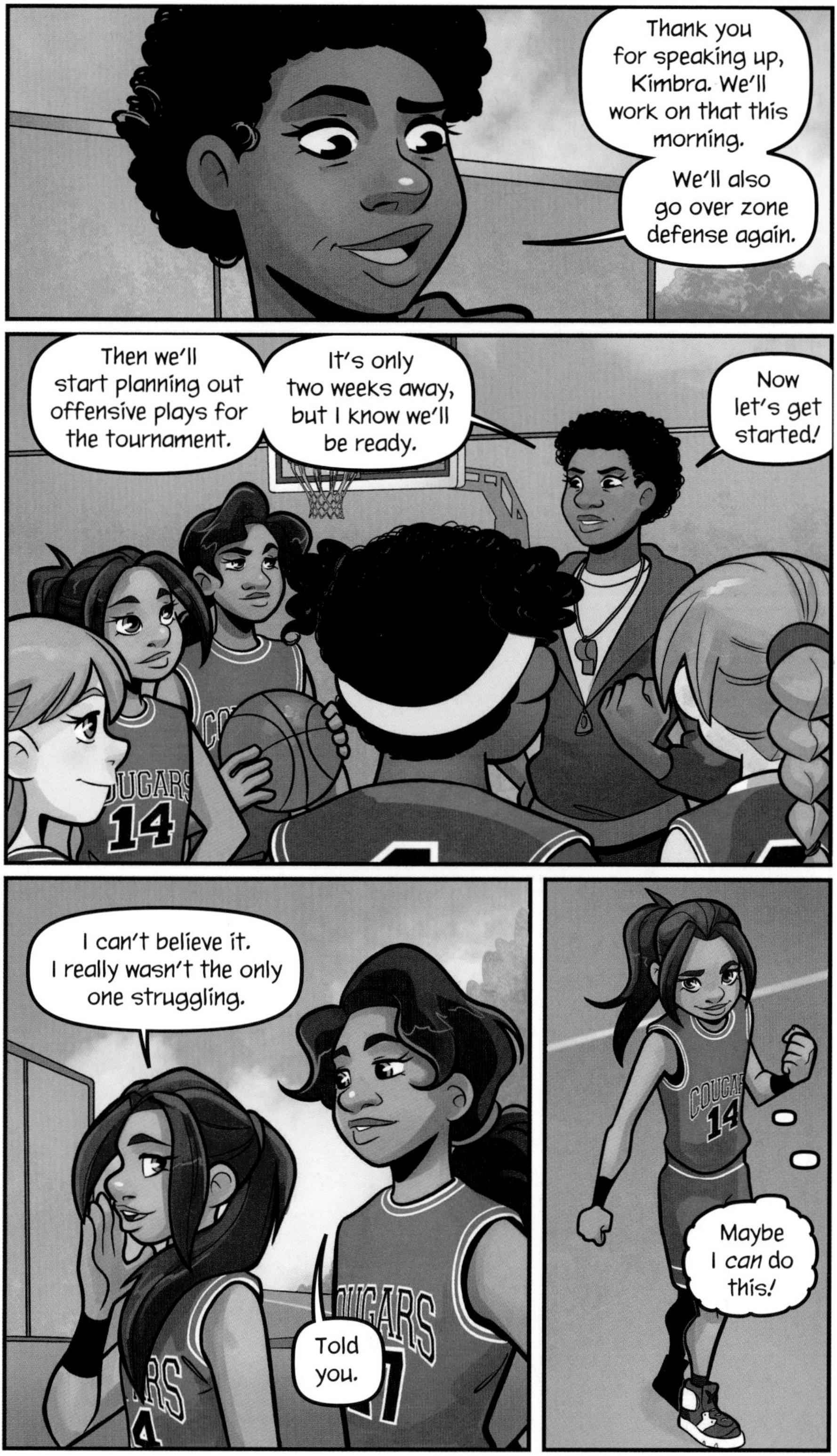
Thank you for speaking up, Kimbra. We'll work on that this morning.
We'll also go over zone defense again.
Then we'll start planning out offensive plays for the tournament.
It's only two weeks away, but I know we'll be ready.
Now let's get started!
COUGARS 14
I can't believe it. I really wasn't the only one struggling.
Told you.
COUGARS 14
Maybe I *can* do this!

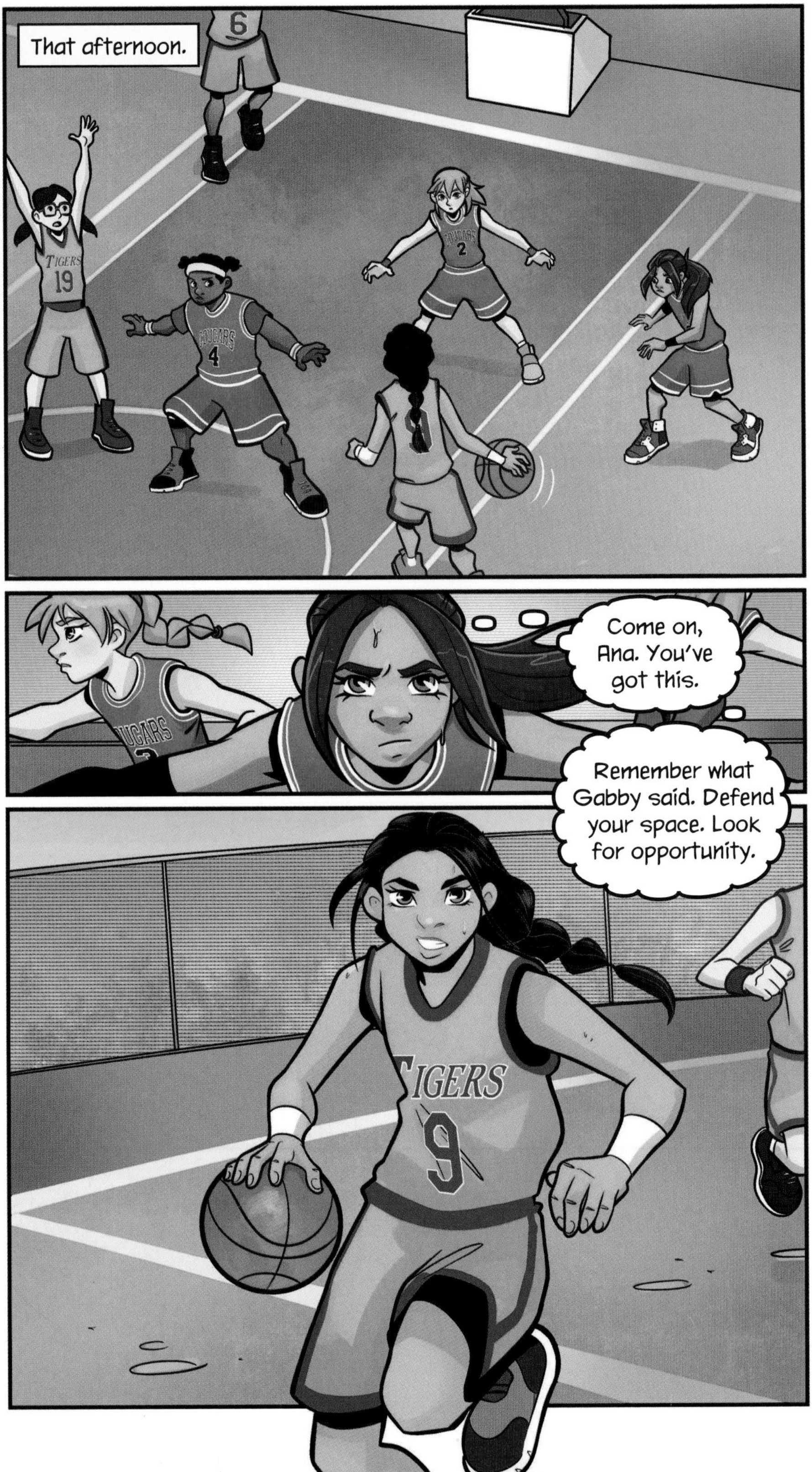
That afternoon.
Come on, Ana. You've got this.
Remember what Gabby said. Defend your space. Look for opportunity.

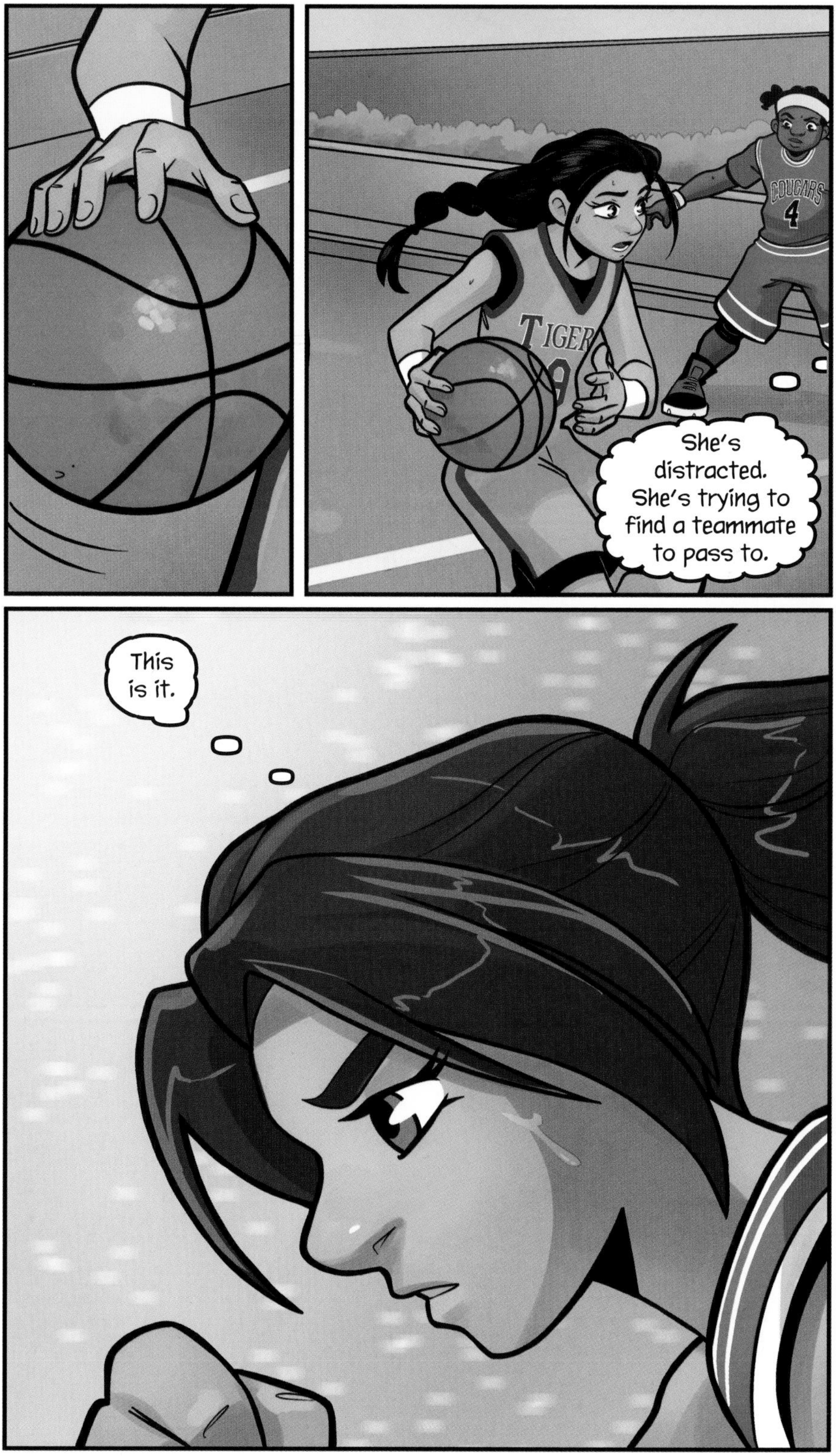
TIGERS
COUGARS 4
She's distracted. She's trying to find a teammate to pass to.
This is it.

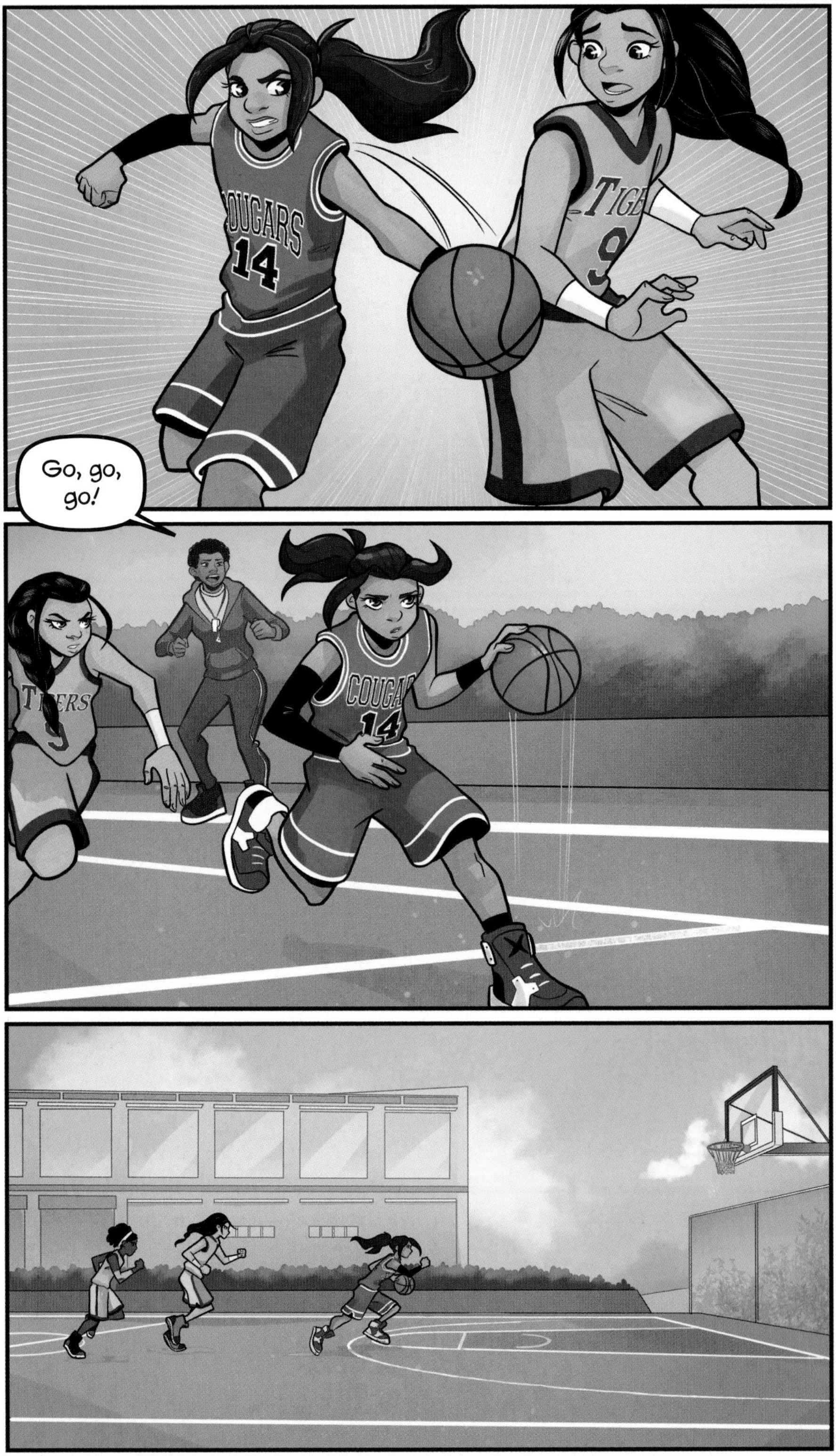
COUGARS 14
TIGE 9
Go, go, go!
TIERS 9
COUGAR 14

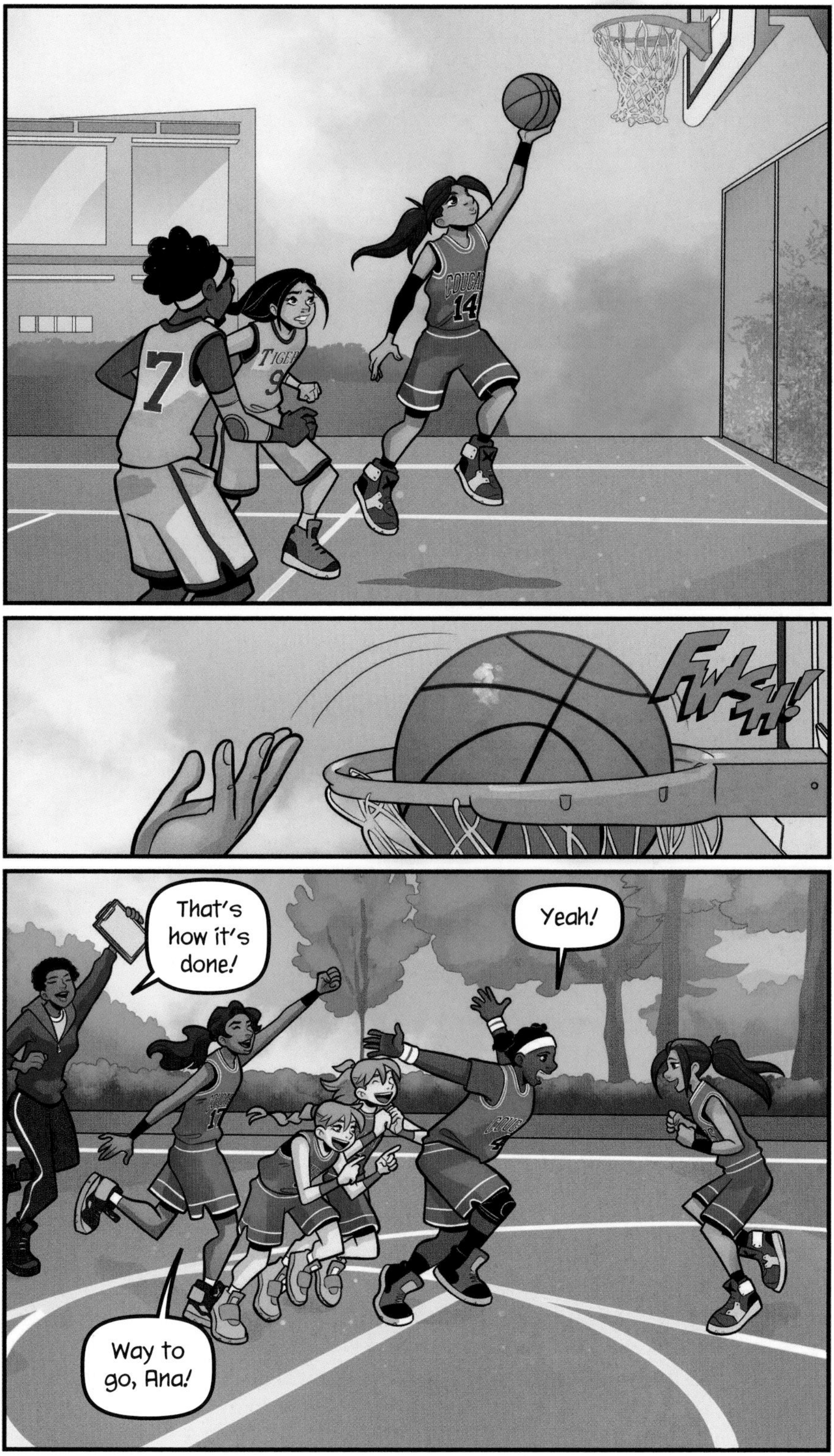
FWSH!
That's how it's done!
Yeah!
Way to go, Ana!

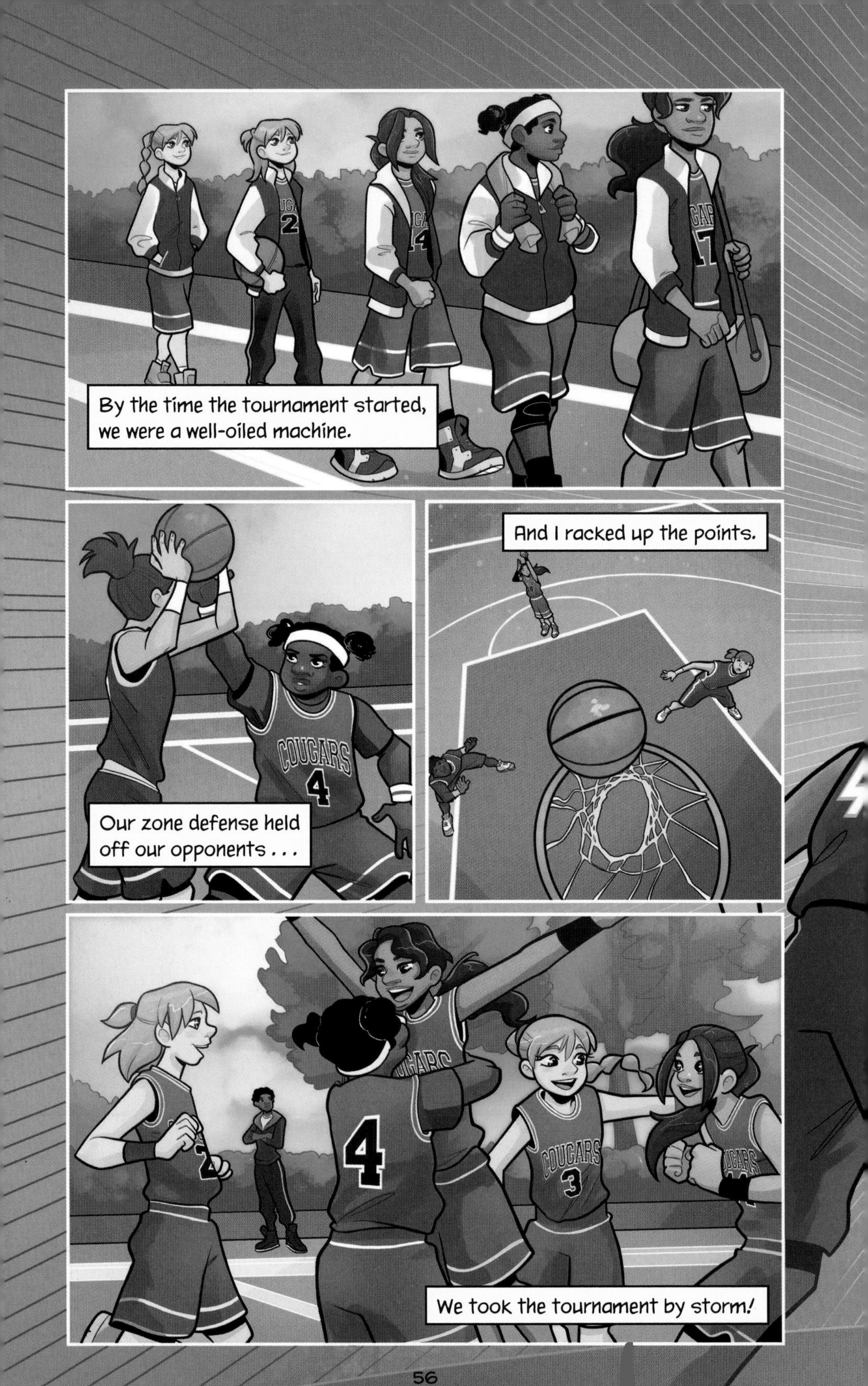

By the time the tournament started, we were a well-oiled machine.
COUGARS
2
14
17
Our zone defense held off our opponents . . .
COUGARS
4
And I racked up the points.
4
COUGARS
3
We took the tournament by storm!

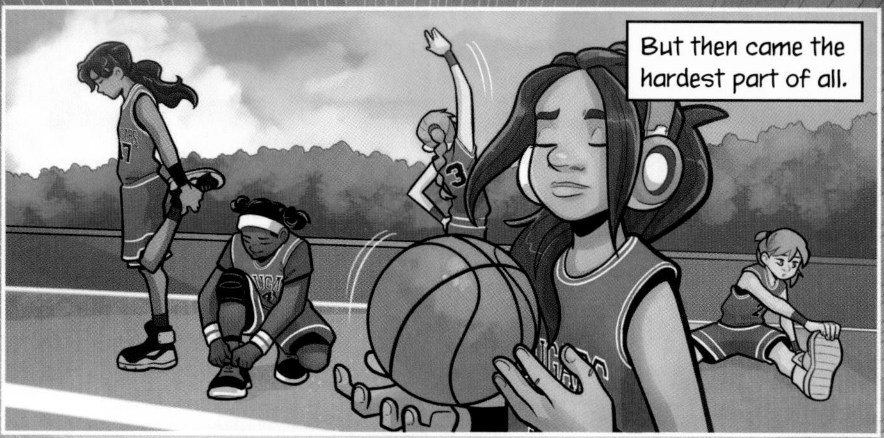
But then came the hardest part of all.

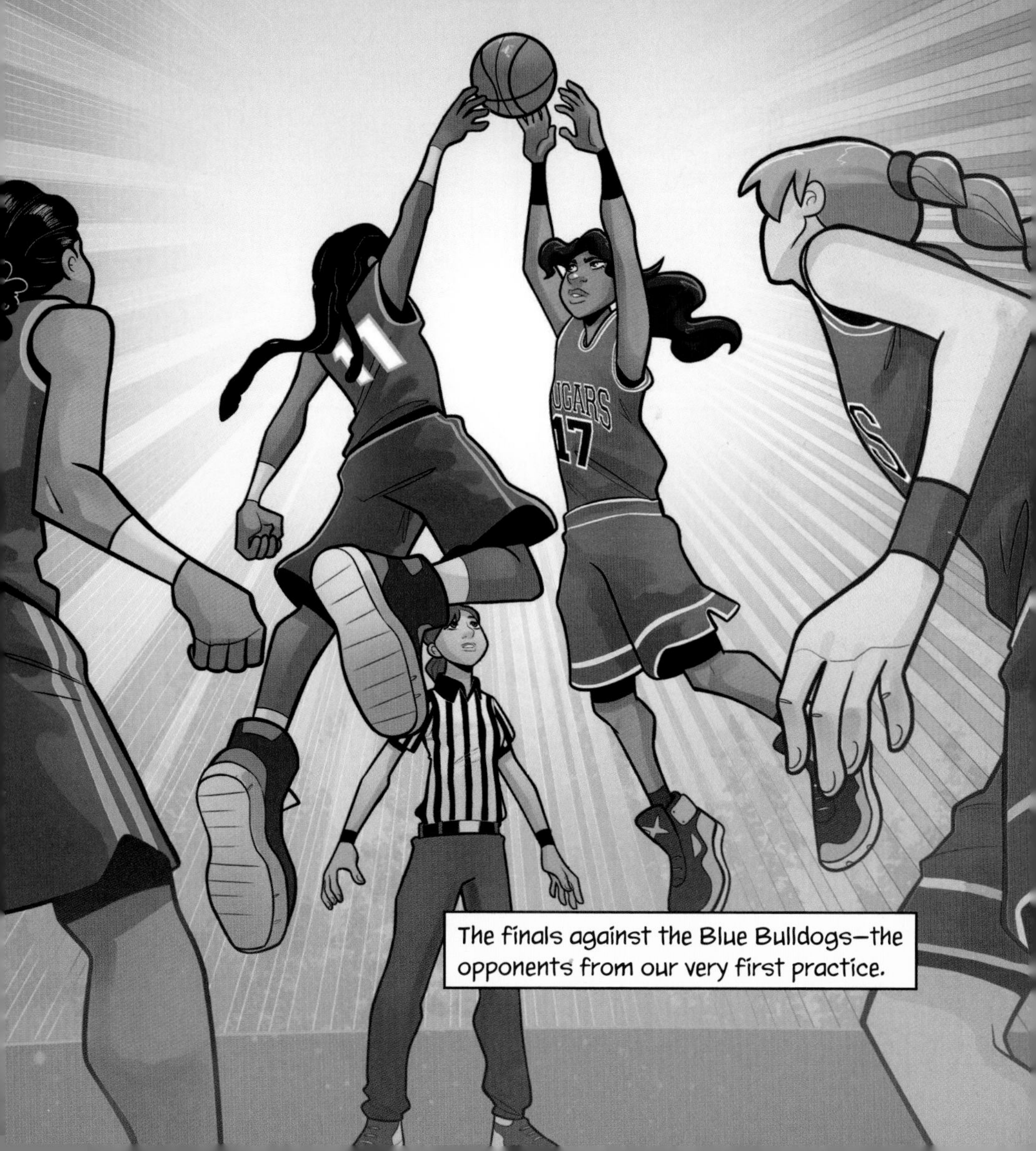
The finals against the Blue Bulldogs—the opponents from our very first practice.

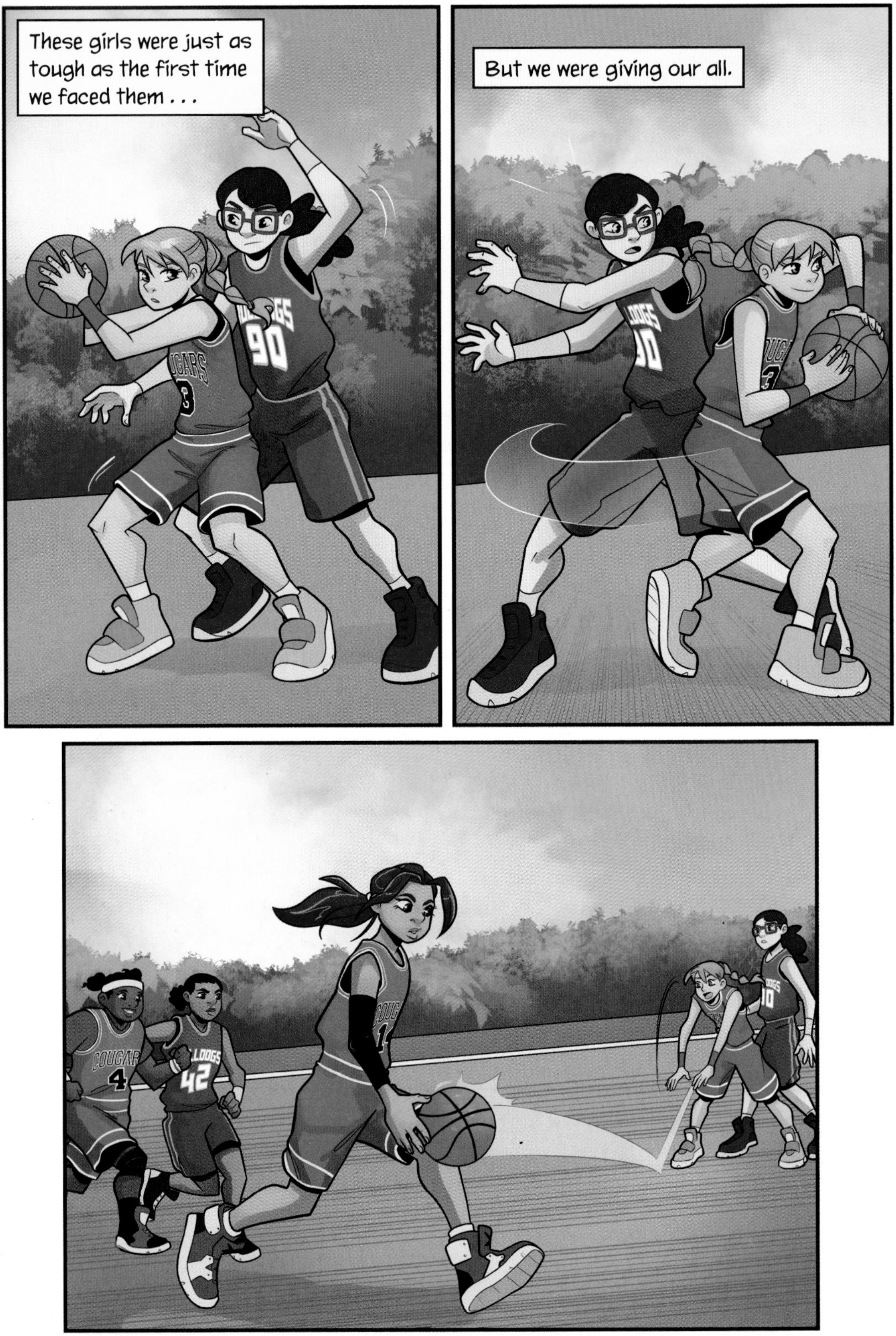
These girls were just as tough as the first time we faced them . . .
But we were giving our all.

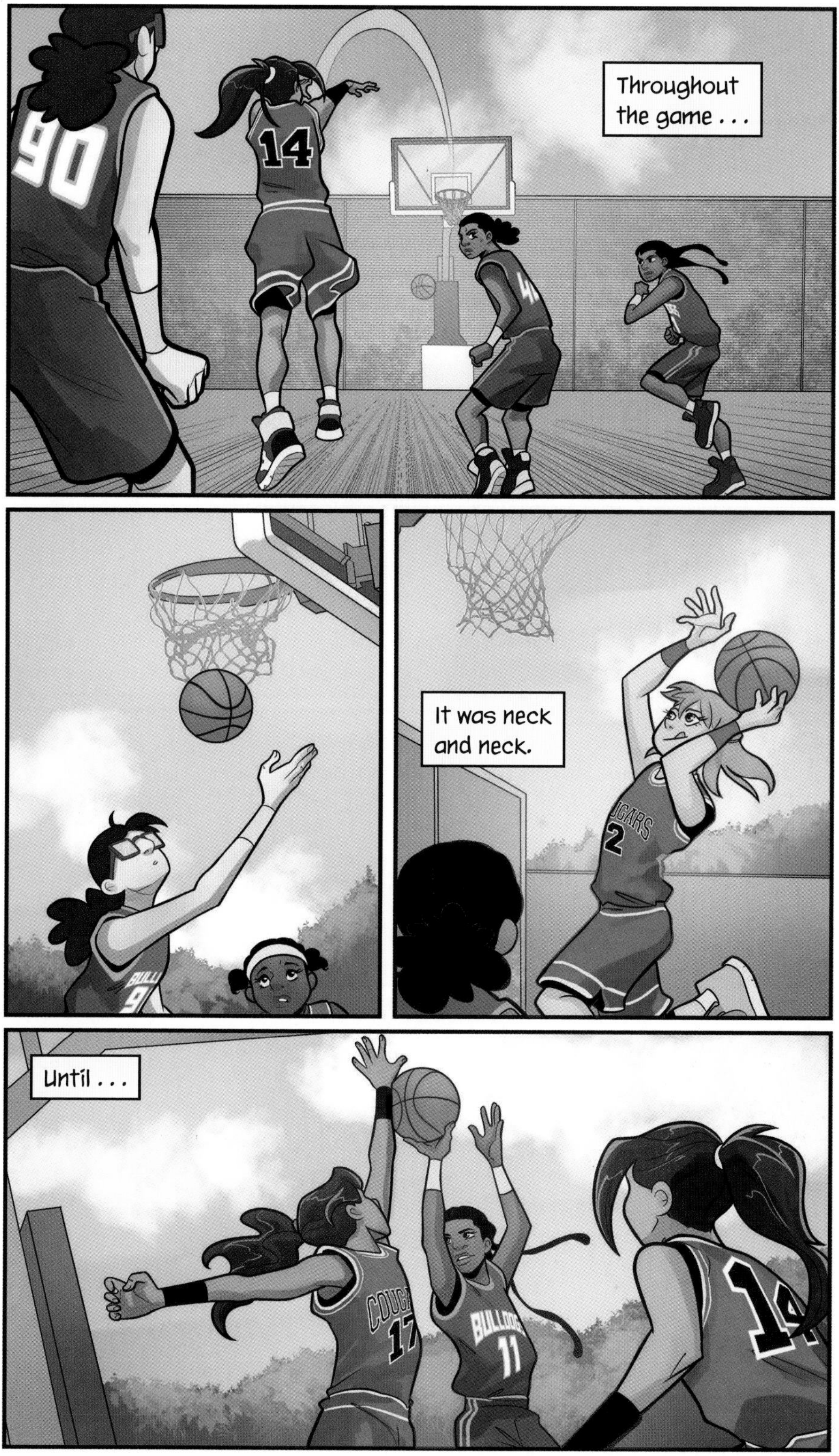
Throughout the game . . .
It was neck and neck.
Until . . .

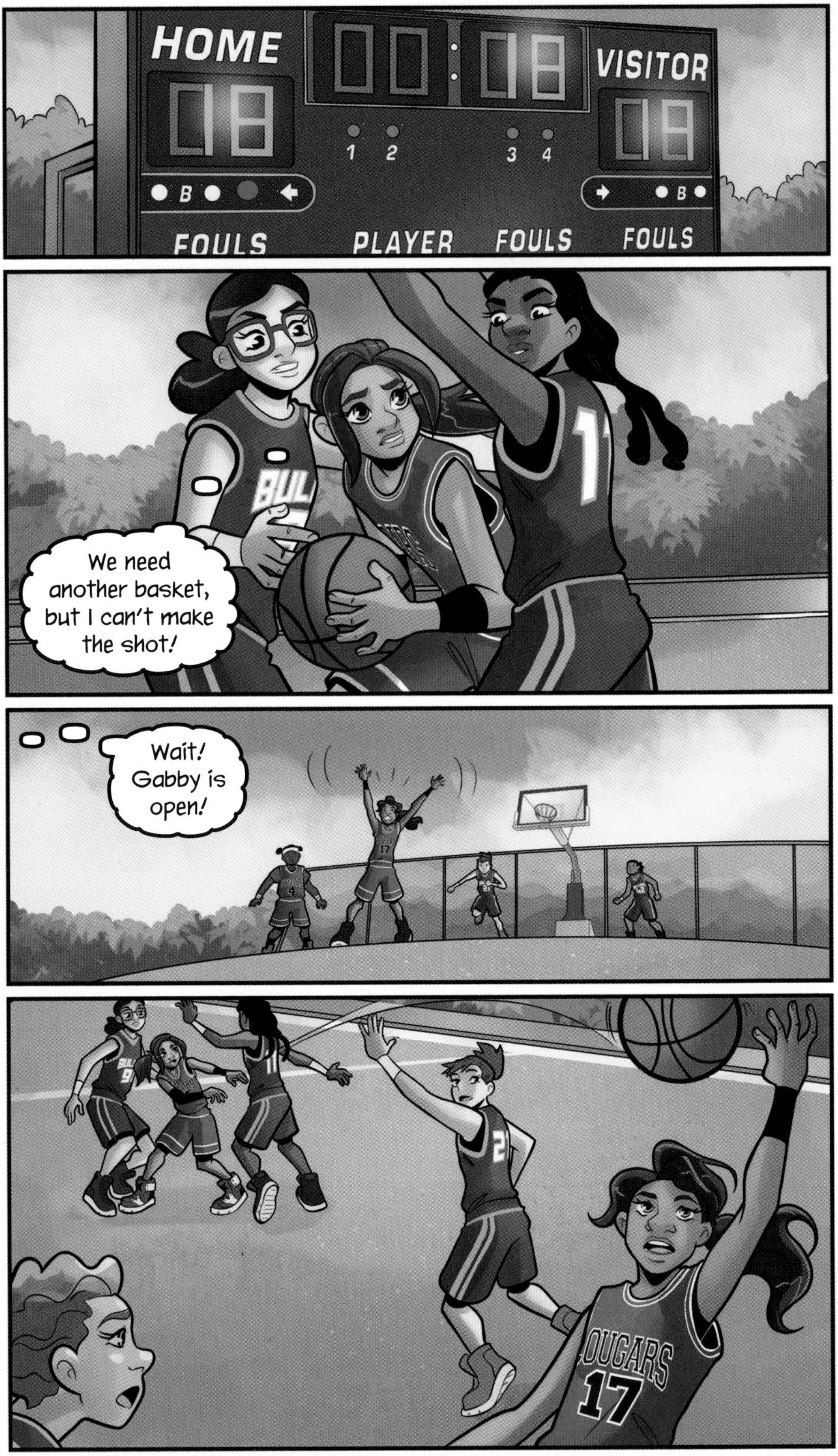
HOME
00:18
VISITOR
18
19
1 2
3 4
B
B
FOULS
PLAYER
FOULS
FOULS
We need another basket, but I can't make the shot!
Wait! Gabby is open!
COUGARS
17

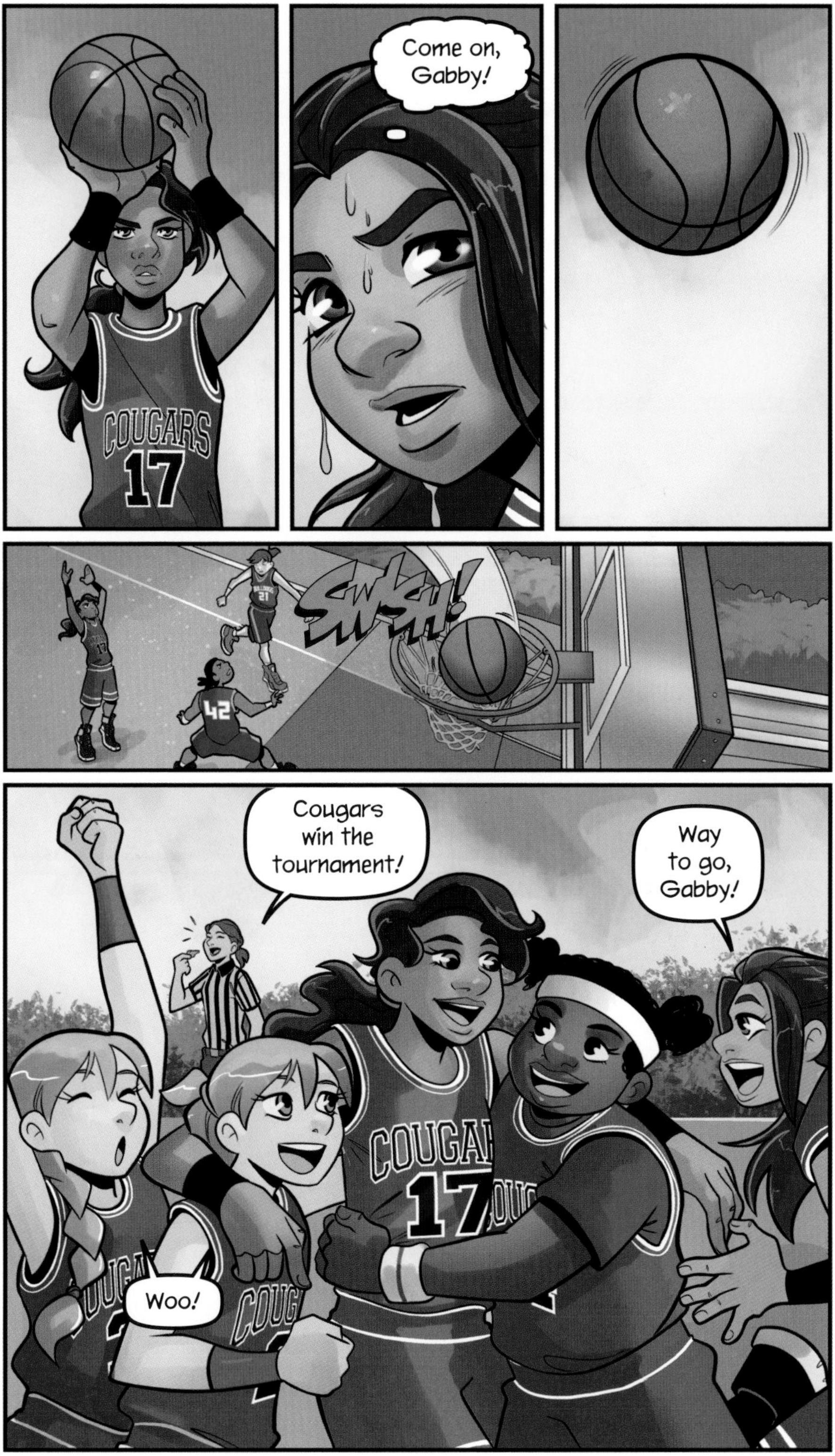
Come on, Gabby!
SWISH!
Cougars win the tournament!
Way to go, Gabby!
Woo!

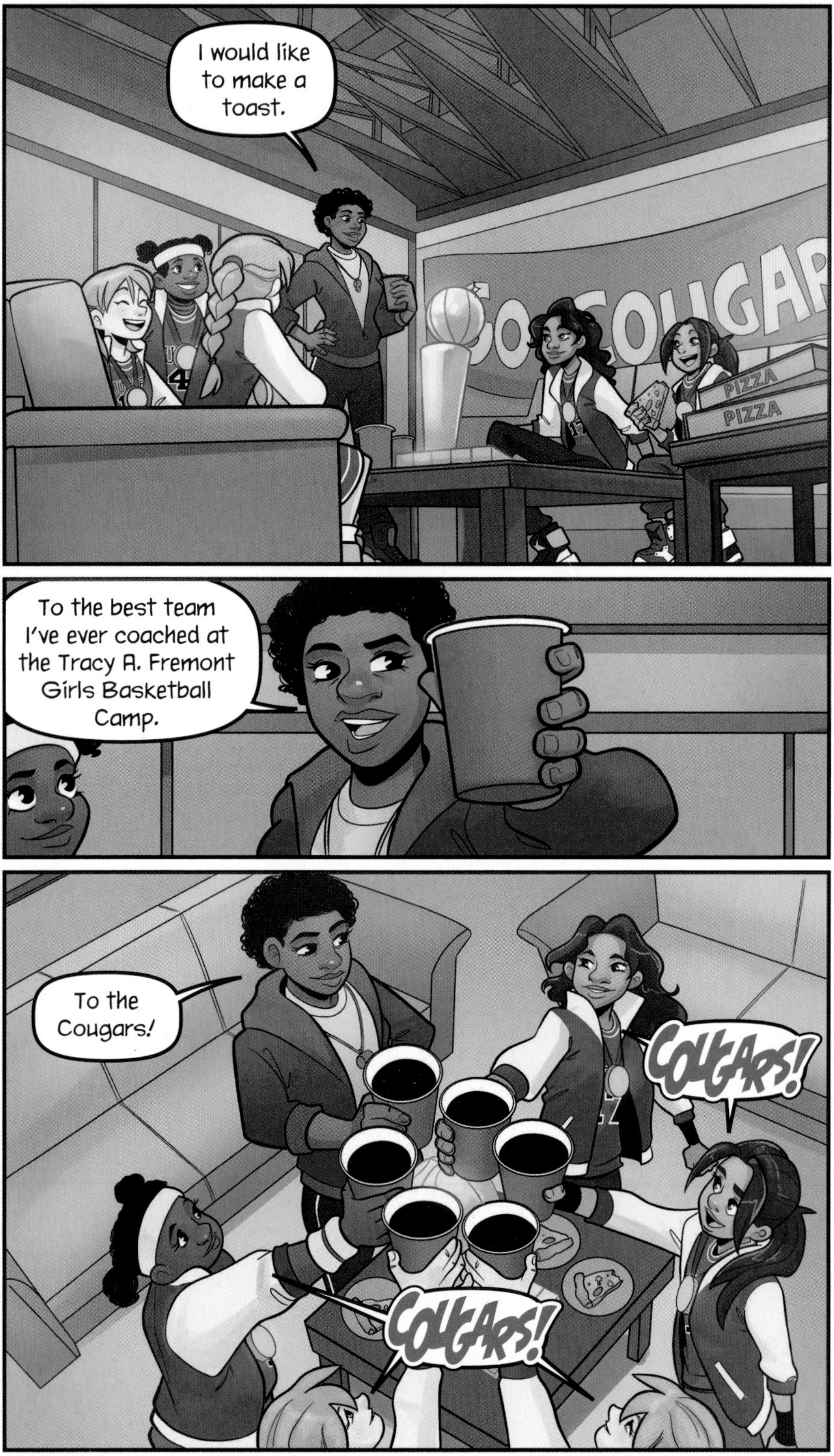
I would like to make a toast.
PIZZA
PIZZA
To the best team I've ever coached at the Tracy A. Fremont Girls Basketball Camp.
To the Cougars!
COUGARS!
COUGARS!

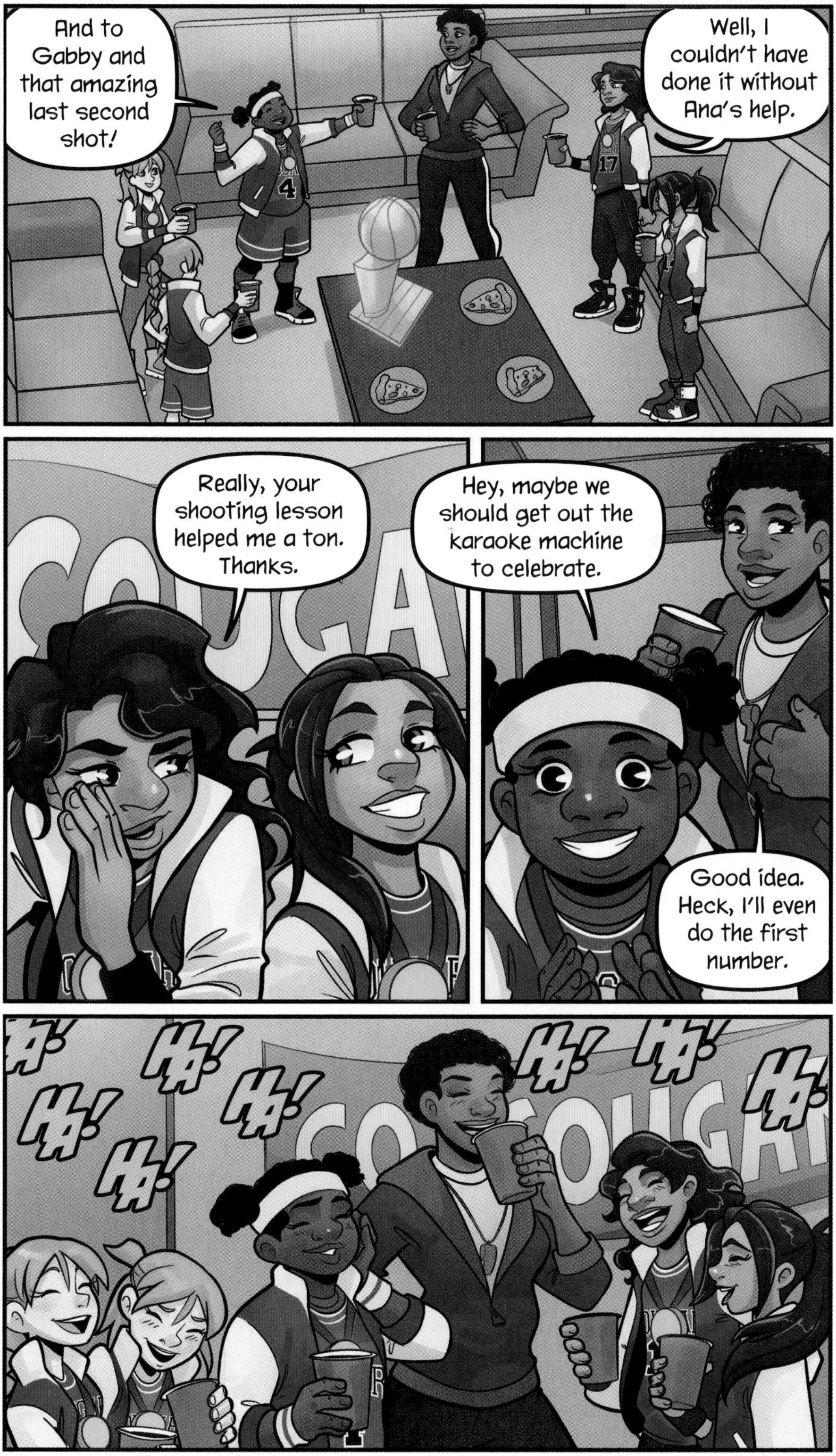
And to Gabby and that amazing last second shot!
Well, I couldn't have done it without Ana's help.
Really, your shooting lesson helped me a ton. Thanks.
Hey, maybe we should get out the karaoke machine to celebrate.
Good idea. Heck, I'll even do the first number.
HA! HA! HA! HA! HA! HA! HA! HA!

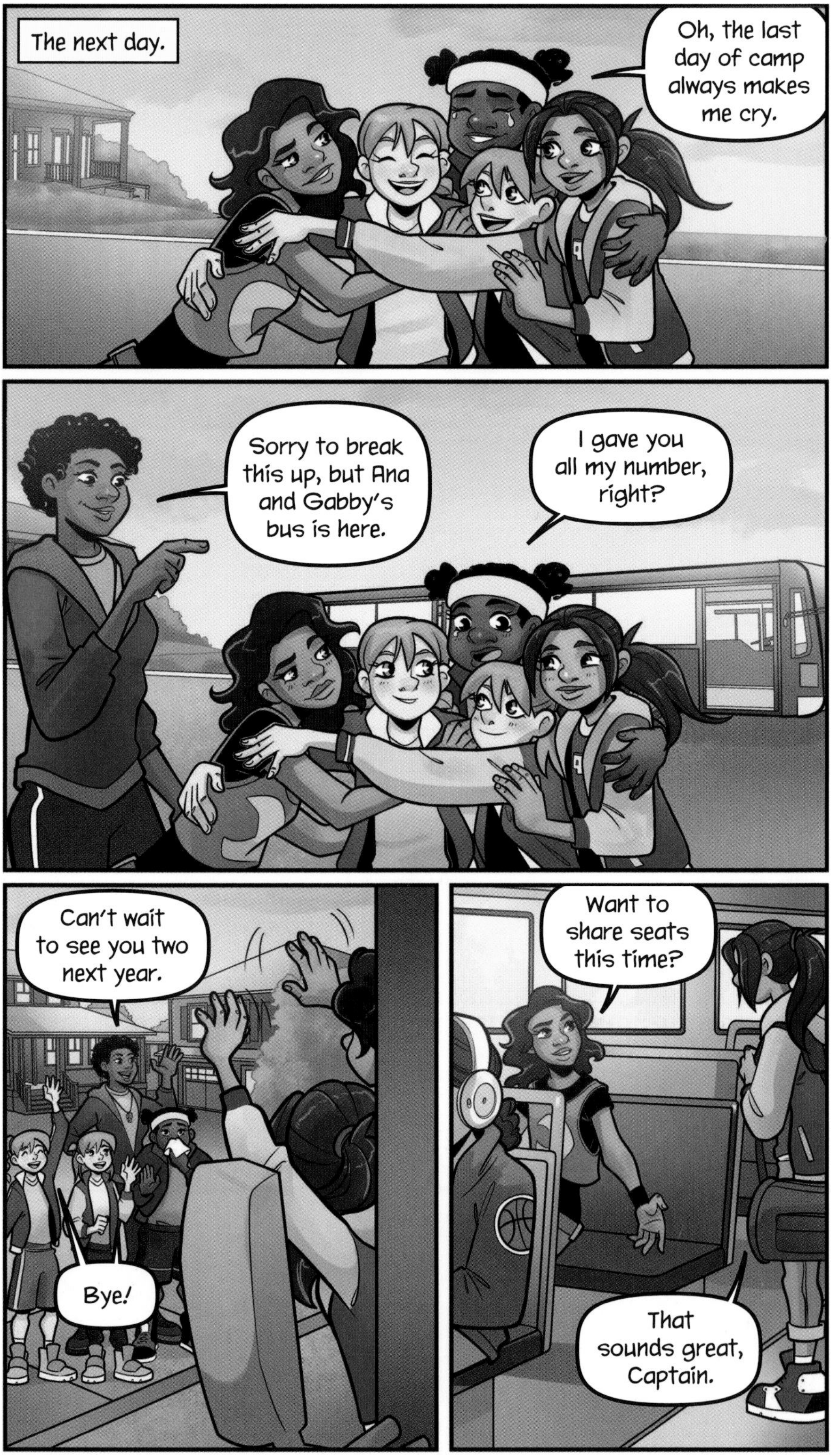
The next day.
Oh, the last day of camp always makes me cry.
Sorry to break this up, but Ana and Gabby's bus is here.
I gave you all my number, right?
Can't wait to see you two next year.
Bye!
Want to share seats this time?
That sounds great, Captain.

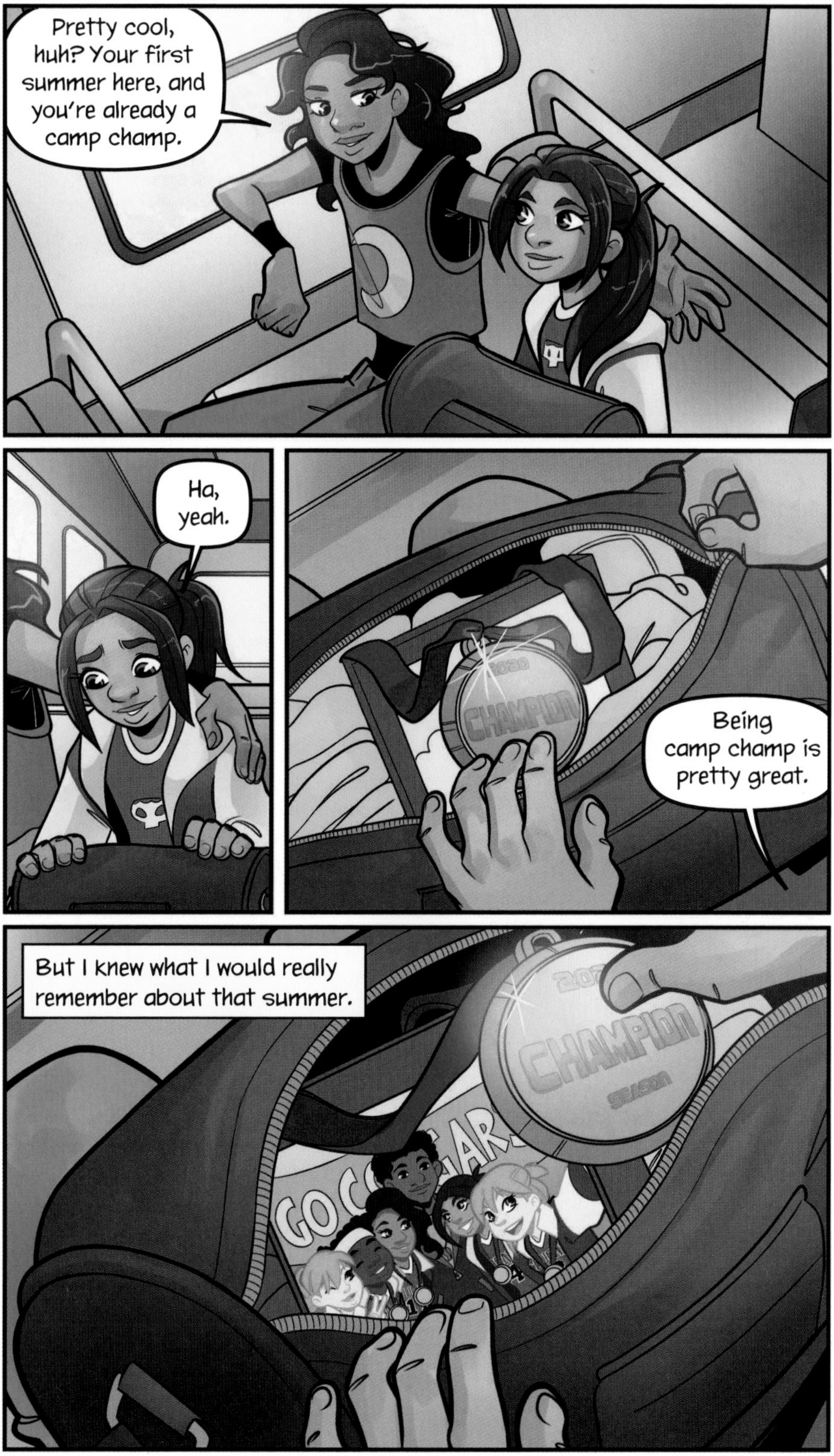
Pretty cool, huh? Your first summer here, and you're already a camp champ.
Ha, yeah.
2020
CHAMPION
Being camp champ is pretty great.
But I knew what I would really remember about that summer.
CHAMPION
SEASON

VISUAL QUESTIONS

1. The border of this panel from page 6 is round and puffy, not straight. Why? When is the scene taking place? Brainstorm other ways you could draw or color the panel to give the same information.

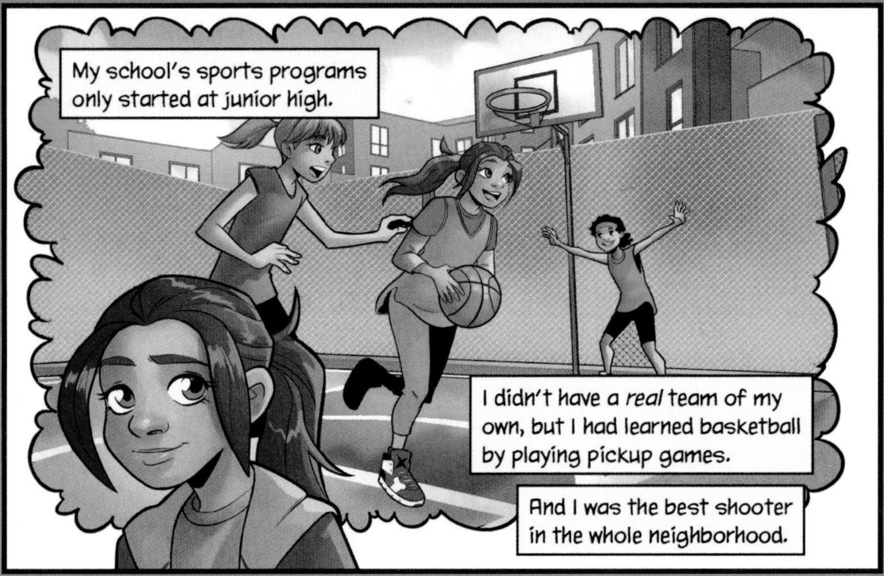

My school's sports programs only started at junior high.
I didn't have a *real* team of my own, but I had learned basketball by playing pickup games.
And I was the best shooter in the whole neighborhood.

2. Why are the words *SLOPPY WORK* near Ana? What feeling does it create? How would it be different if the text wasn't there or just in a thought bubble?

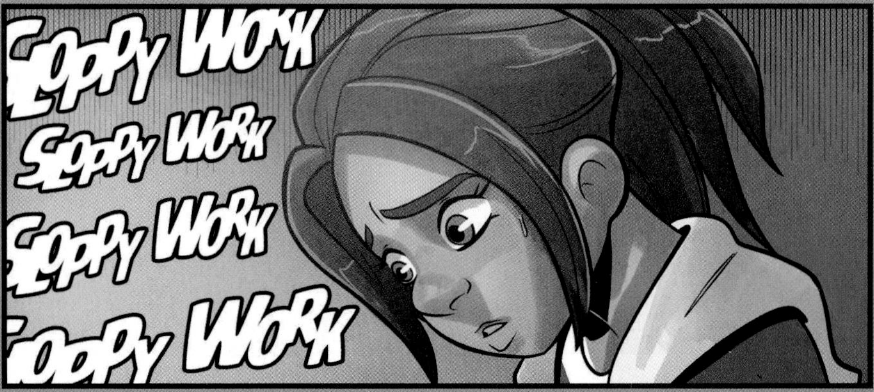

SLOPPY WORK
SLOPPY WORK
SLOPPY WORK
SLOPPY WORK

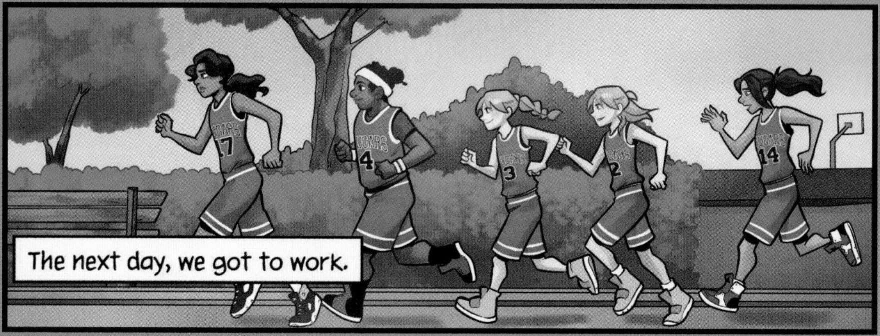
The next day, we got to work.

3. Page 16 summarizes how the whole first morning of practice went in only four panels. This helps move the story along. Try writing out a summary of the practice and be sure to make it just as exciting.

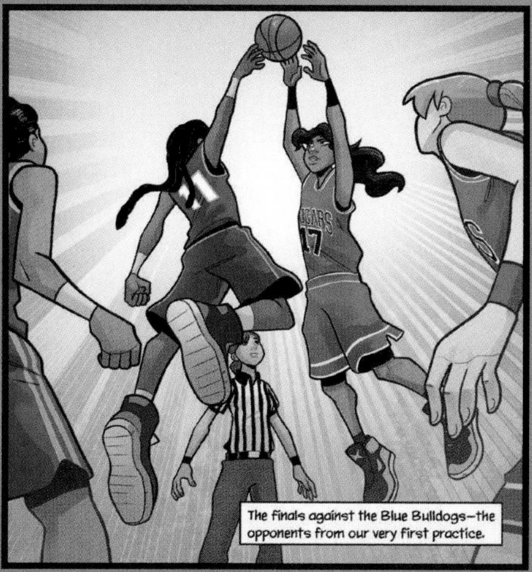
The finals against the Blue Bulldogs—the opponents from our very first practice.

4. The start of the final game on page 57 is an important, exciting moment. How does the art help show that? Look closely and point out at least two specific examples.

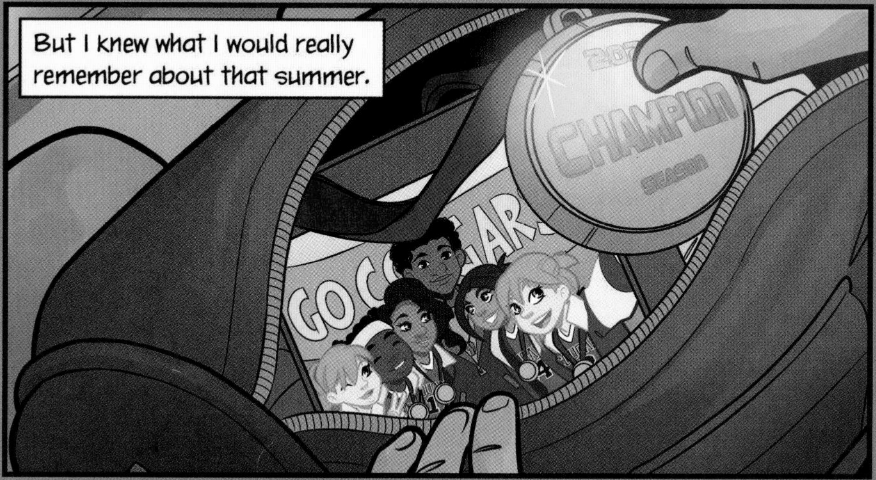
But I knew what I would really remember about that summer.
CHAMPION
SEASON

5. What do you think Ana *will* remember about her summer at camp? She doesn't say, but the art offers clues. Examine the art, then explain your answer.

THE HISTORY OF WOMEN'S BASKETBALL

1891 - Basketball is invented by Canadian American and physical education teacher James Naismith.

1892 - The first women's basketball game is organized by Smith College's Senda Berenson. She changes Naismith's rules to emphasize cooperation and zone playing.

1914 - The American Olympic Committee officially declares it is against women taking part in Olympic competitions.

1926 - The Amateur Athletic Union (AAU) holds the first national basketball tournament for women.

1936 - A women's basketball team called the All-American Red Heads starts traveling across the United States. They compete (and often win) against men's teams. They are a huge hit with crowds.

1955 - The second Pan American Games includes women's basketball as an event.

1976 - Women's basketball becomes an official Olympic sport.

1982 - The first National Collegiate Athletic Association (NCAA) women's basketball tournament is held.

1996 - The National Basketball Association (NBA) establishes the Women's National Basketball Association (WNBA). The league starts with eight teams.

2016 - The WNBA celebrates its 20th season and is now made up of twelve teams.

CHERYL MILLER

Playing in the 1980s, Cheryl Miller was a basketball superstar well before the WNBA was formed. A gold medal Olympian, NCAA champion, and *Sports Illustrated*'s 1985 National Player of the Year, Miller made America think differently about female basketball players.

PAT SUMMITT

University of Tennessee head coach Pat Summitt led her women's team to eight NCAA championships. In her 48-year career from 1974 to 2012, she was the first NCAA coach in any sport to win over 1,000 games with a single team.

CANDACE PARKER

When she was drafted into the WNBA by the Los Angeles Sparks in 2008, Candace Parker made fans take notice. That year, she won both the Rookie of the Year and Most Valuable Player awards. Since then she's become a WNBA champion as well as a two-time Olympic gold medalist. She is one of the WNBA's best players.

GLOSSARY

advice (ad-VISE)—a suggestion about what to do

champ (CHAMP)—short for champion, a person who has won first place

defense (DEE-fens)—when a team doesn't have the ball and is trying to stop points from being scored

distraction (dih-STRAK-shuhn)—something that takes your focus away from other things

free throw (FREE THROH)—an unguarded shot taken from the free-throw line after a foul

offense (AW-fens)—when a team has the ball and is trying to score points

pivot (PIV-uht)—to keep one foot in place on the court while moving the other, usually in order to get in a better position to shoot or pass

play (PLAY)—a specific action in a game

rebound (REE-bound)—the act of getting the basketball after a missed shot

scholarship (SKOL-ur-ship)—a prize or money given to help with a student's education

tactics (TAK-tiks)—a set of plans or actions for reaching a goal

tournament (TUR-nuh-muhnt)—a series of games between several teams that ends with one winner

traveling (TRAV-uh-ling)—the act of moving more than one foot while holding the basketball; traveling is against the rules

zone defense (ZOHN DEE-fens)—a plan for stopping the other team from scoring by having players guard certain areas or "zones" of the court